BLIND TRUST
LAURA SCOTT

🇭 **HARLEQUIN**®LOVE INSPIRED® SUSPENSE

Special thanks and acknowledgment are given to Laura Scott
for her contribution to the True Blue K-9 Unit miniseries.

Recycling programs
for this product may
not exist in your area.

LOVE INSPIRED BOOKS

ISBN-13: 978-1-335-67899-7

Blind Trust

Copyright © 2019 by Harlequin Books S.A.

www.Harlequin.com

Printed in U.S.A.

Hear, O Lord, when I cry with my voice:
have mercy also upon me, and answer me.
–Psalms 27:7

This book is dedicated to Gregory and Marianne Iding, and their chocolate Lab, Moose. It's fun to dog-sit for you when you're on vacation.

ONE

Eva Kendall slowed her pace as she approached the single-story building housing the modest training facility where she worked training guide dogs. Lifting her face to the sky, she basked in the sun warming her skin. June in the Forest Hills area of Queens, New York, could be incredibly hot and humid, but today was the perfect summer day.

Using her key, she entered the training center, thinking about the male chocolate Lab named Cocoa that she would work with this morning. Cocoa was a ten-week-old puppy born to Stella, who was a gift from the Czech Republic to the NYC K-9 Command Unit located in Queens. Most of Stella's pups were being trained as police dogs, but not Cocoa. In less than a month after basic puppy training, Cocoa would be able to go home with Eva to be fostered during his first year of training to become a full-fledged guide dog. Once that year passed, guide dogs like

Cocoa would return to the center to train with their new owners.

A few steps into the building, Eva frowned at the loud thumps interspersed with a cacophony of barking. The raucous noise from the various canines contained a level of panic and fear rather than excitement.

Concerned, she moved quickly through the dimly lit training center to the back hallway, where the kennels were located. Normally she was the first one in every morning, but maybe one of the other trainers had got an early start.

"Hello? Kim, is that you?" Rounding the corner, she paused in the doorway when she saw a tall, heavyset stranger scooping Cocoa out of his kennel, a tire iron lying on the floor beside it. Panic squeezed her chest. "Hey! What are you doing?"

The ferocious barking increased in volume, echoing off the walls and ceiling. The stranger must have heard her. He turned to look at her, then roughly tucked Cocoa under his arm like a football.

"No! Stop!" Panicked, Eva charged toward the man, desperately wishing she had a weapon of some sort.

"Get out of my way," he said in a guttural voice.

"No. Put that puppy down right now!" Eva

stopped and stood her ground, attempting to block his ability to get through the doorway.

"Last chance," he taunted, coming closer.

Fear was bitter on her tongue. She twisted the key ring in her hand, forcing the jagged edges of the keys between her trembling fingers. As he approached, she braced herself, hoping to find a way to stop him. He punched her with his right arm, roughly hitting her shoulder. Pain reverberated down her arm and into her hand, but that didn't stop her from lashing out with the keys, scratching him down the length of his forearm as she tumbled to the ground.

He called her a vile name as he went by, but she didn't care. Ignoring the pain, she surged to her feet and took off after the assailant. Roughly five feet from the doorway leading outside, she lunged, grabbing ahold of the waistband of his black cargo pants and pulling back on it with all her might.

"Stop! Help! Please help! He's stealing a puppy!" She raised her voice, hoping someone outside might overhear.

"Let go!"

No! She couldn't let him get away with Cocoa!

The big and strong assailant dragged her along for a couple of feet before he abruptly turned on her. His meaty forearm, lined with three long, bleeding scratches from her keys, lashed out again, and this time he struck her across the face.

Her head snapped back, sharp pain blooming in her cheek, bringing tears to her eyes and blurring her already diminished vision. The sheer force of the blow knocked her off her feet, and she fell against the wall with a hard thud. Unable to hang on, she released him and slid down along the wall, collapsing on the floor in a crumpled heap. The sound of the puppy's panicked yipping tore at her heart.

"Cocoa," she managed in a choked voice. It was too late. The heavy door leading outside opened and slammed shut with a loud bang.

The assailant was gone, taking her precious puppy—the one she'd hoped to use one day as her own Seeing Eye dog—with him.

Eva forced herself upright. She rushed back to the main reception desk and picked up the phone.

If only she'd got a better look at the guy, she thought, as she dialed the number for the NYC K-9 Command Unit. Her retinitis pigmentosa was already impacting her ability to see clearly. Especially in areas that weren't well lit. The dim interior of the kennels along with his baseball cap had shadowed his face.

With trembling fingers, she clutched the phone to her ear, hoping it wasn't too late to find Cocoa.

"Hey, Gallagher!"

Finn stood and looked over the edge of his cubicle. "What?"

"Pick up line three. Something about a missing dog."

K-9 Officer Finn Gallagher abandoned the notes he was reviewing on Chief Jordan Jameson's murder to pick up the phone. "What's going on?" The NYC K-9 Command Unit headquarters was located in the Jackson Heights area of Queens but served all five boroughs in New York City.

"One of Stella's puppies has just been stolen," Officer Patricia Knowles informed him. Patricia manned the front desk of headquarters, ruling the place with her no-nonsense attitude. "The pup that's missing is Cocoa, the one donated to the guide dog program."

"Stolen?" Finn scowled and glanced down at his yellow Labrador retriever, Abernathy. His K-9 partner's specialty was search and rescue, fitting for finding a stolen puppy. Finn clipped a leash onto Abernathy. All the K-9s were named after fallen K-9 officers, and his was no exception. Abernathy was named in honor of Michael Abernathy, who was killed in the line of duty while trying to rescue a child from his suicidal father. The child had survived, but Officer Abernathy had been hit in the cross fire and ultimately died. "I'm on it. Thanks." He hung up the phone. "Come, Abernathy."

Wearing his K-9 vest identifying him as a law enforcement officer, Abernathy was all business, keeping pace beside Finn as he left the K-9 Unit headquarters. The guide dog training center was located in Forest Hills, a ten-to-fifteen-minute drive from Jackson Heights. Finn opened the back of his white K-9 SUV for Abernathy and then slid in behind the wheel.

Rush hour made the ride to the training center take longer than he'd hoped. A beautiful blonde hovered just inside the doorway, anxiously waiting for him.

With Abernathy at his side, he assessed the woman. She appeared to be in her late twenties, her heart-shaped face and stunningly beautiful features framed by long straight blond hair. He scowled as he noticed she was holding an ice pack against a dark bruise marring her cheek. She stepped back and gestured for him to come inside.

"I'm Officer Finn Gallagher. What happened?" he asked with concern. "You were assaulted? I was told that Stella's puppy has been stolen."

The blonde offered a lopsided smile. "I'm Eva Kendall, and I'm the one who reported the puppy-napping."

"You're hurt. I'll call an ambulance." Finn reached for his radio.

"No need," Eva said quickly. "It's more important to find Cocoa."

Finn knew Cocoa was a chocolate Lab. A valuable animal, sure, but worth stealing? He had to believe the other guide dogs at the facility might be worth just as much, maybe more. He looked at Eva. "Tell me what happened."

She moved the ice pack so she could speak, and he was struck anew by her clear porcelain skin and brilliant blue eyes. He did his best to avoid being distracted by her beauty, focusing on her story. "I came in early to work with Cocoa. The minute I entered the building, I heard thumps and loud barking from the dogs. I feared something was wrong, so I headed back toward the kennels."

"Alone?"

She lifted a shoulder, then winced as if the motion hurt. "I convinced myself that it was nothing, until I found a stranger grabbing Cocoa from his kennel."

Finn clenched his jaw, imagining the scenario. Was it possible the chocolate Lab had been targeted on purpose?

"I shouted at him to stop, but he didn't listen." Distress darkened Eva's blue eyes. "He punched me in the shoulder, knocking me to the floor, but I managed to scratch him with my keys." She gestured to the key ring sitting on the counter. "I thought you might be able to get a DNA sample from them."

He lifted a brow, secretly impressed she'd thought of that. "We can try. Go on, what happened next?"

"I ran after him and grabbed him from behind, but he hit me again and got away."

Hearing that the perp had hit her twice had him grinding his teeth in a flash of anger. It deeply bothered him when men used their strength against women. "Are you sure about not calling an ambulance? I think it's best if you get checked out at the ER."

"I'm fine." Eva waved a hand dismissively. "I've been hurt worse tussling with my older sister. We used to wrestle a lot when we were younger."

"Your older sister?" Finn felt a bit confused by the change in topic.

"Yes." Eva's gaze reflected a deep sorrow. "Unfortunately, Malina died three weeks ago when she was struck by a car."

"I'm sorry to hear that." He wanted to offer comfort but told himself to focus on the issue at hand. "I have to ask about the attack. Did the guy look at all familiar?"

"No. But I still don't understand. Why steal a puppy? Especially since we have older dogs here, too. Although it's possible the older dogs might try to bite more than a puppy would."

"Good question." He flipped his notebook shut and cast his gaze around the interior of the building. "Take me along the assailant's path. I'll also need to review the security video."

"The video won't be available until my boss

gets in, I don't know how to use the equipment. But aren't you going to head out to try to find him?" Eva asked, exasperation ringing in her voice. "I specifically asked for a search-and-rescue team."

Finn flashed a wry grin. "Abernathy is the best search-and-rescue K-9 on the force, and, yes, I plan to head out to search for Cocoa. But I need to see the path the guy took, and I need something belonging to either the perp or Cocoa to use, as well."

Mollified, Eva wheeled around and led the way back through the training center. "There's a tire iron on the floor near the kennel. I think he used it to break inside the building then dropped it here by the kennel."

Finn took note of the tire iron on the floor. Metal wasn't the best substance to use for obtaining a scent, but Abernathy was exceptionally smart. "Don't touch anything," he warned. "We may be able to use the tire iron or the keys to pick up the perp's scent."

"I won't."

He went back to put the keys in an evidence bag, then led his K-9 partner to the tire iron. He pointed at the object and offered the evidence bag of keys as two ways for the animal to pick up the scent. "Find, Abernathy," he commanded.

The yellow Lab sniffed along the entire length of the tire iron, going back and forth as if to distinguish the smell of the metal compared to the person who'd held it, and then buried his nose in the evidence bag.

"Find," Finn repeated. Abernathy put his nose to the ground and began following the scent. Finn let his K-9 take the lead, following his partner as the dog made his way from the kennel out to the main corridor toward the main entrance, alerting at several spots along the way.

"He's on the trail," Eva said excitedly.

"He is," Finn agreed, energized by his K-9's ability to track the perp. "Stay here. We'll be back shortly."

"Wait! I want to come with you." She tossed the ice pack on the counter and hurried to catch up with him. She didn't like leaving the place unlocked and hoped they wouldn't go too far.

"We work better alone," he protested.

"I'm coming. If we find Cocoa, he'll be scared to death, but he knows me. Cocoa might even respond to the sound of my voice." She sent him a frustrated glance. "Come on, Officer Gallagher. Stop wasting time. Let's go!"

"Call me Finn," he told her. Giving up, he reluctantly allowed Eva to tag along as he and Abernathy went to work. The K-9 alerted at the doorway leading out the main entrance, then turned to the left as he followed the perp's scent.

Eva didn't say anything but seemed to watch in awe as Abernathy alerted again a short while later. They went one block, then a second, the K-9 picking up the scent at regular intervals.

"Good boy," Finn encouraged his partner, giving him a nice rub as a reward for his good work. Then he straightened. "Find, Abernathy."

The yellow Lab put his nose back to the ground, sniffing and moving in a circular and seemingly random pattern. Abernathy made a circle and then came back, alerting on the same spot he had before.

"I guess this is it." Finn battled a wave of disappointment that their attempt to find Cocoa had come to such a quick end. He glanced back the way they had come. Three blocks. The perp had clearly gone in this direction for at least three blocks. "Abernathy has lost the scent, here at the intersection in front of the Grocer's Best convenience store."

"Maybe we could go up a block or two, just to be sure?" Eva suggested.

Finn nodded. "I'll take him a few blocks each way."

Twenty minutes later, Finn knew it was no use. The attempt to pick up the perp's scent had failed. Abernathy didn't alert once.

"It's likely the guy had a car waiting here for him," he told her as they walked back to the training center. "Otherwise, Abernathy would have picked up his scent."

"I guess I hadn't thought of that," Eva acknowledged, her slim shoulders slumping in defeat. Then she brightened. "Maybe we'll be able to catch the vehicle make, model and license plate number from the video."

Again he was impressed with her cop-like instincts. Most of the women he'd dated—of which there had been many, although no one serious—didn't have a clue about what law enforcement really entailed. He looked up at the security cameras posted on the outside corners of the training center building. "Maybe, but it will depend on the camera range and the quality of the lens. It would be a huge break if we could get something from the tapes. How soon can I check it out?"

Eva shrugged, then winced, putting a hand on her injured shoulder. "As soon as Wade gets in."

"Your boss?"

She nodded, her straight long blond hair shimmering in the sunlight. "Wade Yost is the director in charge of the guide dog training center. He reports to the owner."

"Have you seen anyone lurking around over the past few days?" Finn asked. "The fact that this guy broke in through the back door, makes me think he cased the center before deciding to grab Cocoa."

"No, I haven't noticed anyone. Although maybe the security video will give us that information, too."

"How far back do they go?"

She pursed her lips. "I'm not sure. Maybe a week or two? I know they run on loops."

Two weeks wasn't very long, but he'd take what he could get. "Do you think you'd recognize the guy if you saw him again?"

"I'm not sure." Eva looked away, gazing off into the distance. "Maybe."

Her tone lacked conviction, but he wasn't deterred. "Tell you what. How about you work with a sketch artist to give us an idea of what this guy might look like? Witnesses are always surprised at how much they remember."

"I don't know," she hedged. "I don't think it will help. I honestly didn't get a good look at his face." Her lack of enthusiasm toward working with the sketch artist bothered him. Where was the woman who had insisted on coming with him to find Cocoa?

"Give it a try," he persisted. "It can't hurt."

There was a long pause before she gave a curt nod. "Okay. But please don't pin all your hopes on the sketch. The keys I used to scratch him with will likely help more than the brief glimpse I got of him."

"DNA takes time, and if this guy isn't already in the system, having it won't help until we get a suspect to use as a potential match. The sketch is a better place to start."

"Okay."

He held the door of the training center open for

her, wondering once again why Cocoa had been targeted. The pup was only ten weeks old—what was the point of stealing him? Especially since there were other, more valuable dogs in the kennel?

Did someone have a grudge against the training center? Had the pup been taken as a way to ruin their reputation? He made a mental note to ask Wade Yost for a list of employees who had been fired in the past year.

Finn waited fifteen minutes before Wade showed up. The director was roughly five feet eight inches tall with a husky build. He had dirty-blond hair and nondescript features.

"Eva? What happened? How did you let Cocoa get away?" Yost demanded.

"I tried my best to prevent it," Eva said. "I'm sorry."

"The man attacked her," Finn said, speaking up on her behalf. He shot the director of the training facility a narrow glare. "She's fortunate she wasn't seriously injured or killed."

"Yes, of course," Yost said, backpedaling. "Eva, I'm so sorry you were hurt. Do you want to take the rest of the day off?"

Finn glanced at her and she rubbed a hand over her shoulder.

"Maybe. But first Officer Gallagher wants to see the security video."

"Yes, I do," Finn said. "And you don't seem to have a security system, correct?"

"With all the dogs in here, didn't think I'd need one." Wade Yost led the way to his office and the computer screens he had sitting on a table in the corner. The director went over and pulled up the video feed, going back a few hours. There was no sound from the video, and a heavy silence fell among them as they watched.

Finn rested his hand on Abernathy's silky head. He saw Eva entering the guide dog training facility through the front door. The cameras were only on the outside of the building, not on the inside. They waited, watching various cars driving by on the street, as the timer clicked through. Nine minutes later, the door abruptly swung open and a man dressed in black rushed out. The guy instantly turned left, the same way Abernathy had tracked him, then disappeared from view. The man's face was averted, a ball cap pulled low on his forehead as if he'd known exactly where the camera was located.

"Do you have another camera?" Finn asked. "Something pointing down the street?"

"Afraid not," Yost said. "The other camera points to the parking lot in the back of the building."

"That might show him breaking in," Eva pointed out.

Yost went to work pulling up that security feed.

As Finn watched, he could see a tall man wearing black from head to toe, along with the baseball hat pulled over his brow, coming out from behind a dumpster. He again kept his head down as he made his way to the back door. Using the tire iron, he opened it up and disappeared inside. Once again, the angle of the camera made it impossible to see his face beneath the rim of the cap.

Finn blew out a frustrated breath. "I want copies of the video going as far back as you have it."

"Should be about a week's worth," Yost said. "Maybe eight days at the max."

Great, that was just great. The video they had wasn't helpful, and Eva hadn't got a good look at the guy. He'd still have Eva work with a sketch artist, but at this point they had very few clues.

Finn turned toward Eva's boss. "Tell me, do you have a list of employees who were let go in the past twelve months?"

"Uh, yeah, sure." Yost looked uncomfortable as he glanced at Eva, then back at Finn. "I'll, um, get that for you."

Yost rummaged around in his desk drawer, then pulled out a sheet of paper. He glanced again at Eva before handing it over. "You'll, uh, keep that confidential, won't you?" he asked.

"Of course." Finn didn't understand why the

guy was so uncomfortable until he scanned the list, his gaze stumbling across a familiar name.

Malina Kendall-Stallings.

Eva's older sister.

TWO

Eva could feel Finn's intense gaze boring into her and desperately wished she could see him more clearly. Unfortunately, he was standing with his back to the large window overlooking the street, and the light coming in behind him cast a shadow over his face.

"Is something wrong?" she asked, finally breaking the strained silence.

"No, of course not." Carefully, Finn folded the paper her boss had given him and tucked it into his pocket. "Wade, do you mind if I take Eva down to the station with me? I'd like her to work with a sketch artist. We need all the help we can get identifying this assailant in order to get Cocoa back."

"That's fine," Wade agreed. "Eva, why don't you take the rest of the day off? You were planning to leave early anyway, right?"

"Yes, I was." Normally working with the animals relaxed her, but since her brother-in-law,

Pete Stallings, had just left town to attend a conference, she needed to pick up her three-year-old nephew, Mikey, from his preschool program. Spending extra time with him would be nice. The poor little boy was struggling after his mother's death just three weeks ago.

She picked up her purse from the counter, wishing there was a way to get out of going with Finn. She really didn't want to work with the police sketch artist, knowing that what little she'd been able to see of the man wasn't enough to recreate a good likeness. Yet she wasn't about to reveal her degenerative eyesight issues to Finn Gallagher, either. She knew only too well that men treated her differently once they discovered the truth. Sure, her ex-fiancé, Rafe Del Rosa, had denied breaking off their relationship because of her diagnosis, but she knew the truth.

Rafe was an artist and the ability to see was very important to him. The fact that one day she wouldn't be able to see or appreciate his work had bothered him. Considering they'd met at one of his art exhibits, she could somewhat understand.

Despite what she'd heard on the rare times her parents had taken them to church, love did not conquer all.

Losing Rafe, her sister, Malina, and all too soon her vision had been three life-changing events too many. She'd turned away from the church, unable to believe that all of this adversity was part of God's plan.

There was no plan. Wasn't she living proof of that?

"Eva? Are you ready to go? Joey, our sketch artist, will meet us there."

She realized Finn and his yellow Lab, Abernathy, were hovering near the main entrance, waiting for her. She shook off her depressing thoughts and moved toward him.

She wasn't blind yet. She cleared her throat. "How far away is the K-9 headquarters?"

"In Jackson Heights. Don't worry, I can drive you home afterward." Finn held the door open, and in the bright sunlight she was able to see him more clearly. Earlier, she'd been too worried about Cocoa to notice, but now she could see just how broad Finn's shoulders were and how handsome he was. His dark brown hair was longer than most cops she knew generally wore it, a lock falling over his forehead and his green eyes were incredible. There was a tiny part of her that wanted to take the time to memorize his features so she could picture him in her mind's eye forever, but she gave herself a mental shake.

A relationship was out of the question. In a few years she'd be deemed legally blind. Her diagnosis was such that her field of vision would narrow over the next few years, until she could only see through a small circle. She'd already accepted the fact that she'd spend the rest of her life alone. At least she had her nephew, Mikey, to help care for. And the dogs she trained were also important to her.

She didn't need anyone else.

"Where do you live?" Finn asked.

"Not far. I don't need a ride home, but maybe you could bring me back here to the training center. I live a short subway ride away."

"We'll see," Finn said, his tone noncommittal. She sensed he wasn't the type to take no for an answer, but she didn't need his help.

Remaining independent was very important to her. No way was she going to start leaning on a man now. The more she took the same route to and from work, the better she'd be able to navigate once her eyesight vanished for good. Granted, she'd have a guide dog of her own by then, but still it was important to establish a routine so she could continue to work. Who better to train guide dogs than a blind woman?

Finn opened the back of the police SUV so Abernathy could get into the back. Then he came around and opened the passenger-side door for her.

"Thanks," she said, sliding inside.

"Not a problem." Finn closed the door behind her, and instantly she became aware of the musky scent of his aftershave, which seemed to permeate the interior of the vehicle.

"You mentioned your sister passed away three weeks ago. What happened?"

The change of subject was odd, but she sensed he was making small talk. "Malina was hit by a car and killed on impact. It's been a difficult time for all of us—her husband, Pete, and their little boy, Mikey."

"I'm sorry to hear that." Finn paused, then asked, "Did your sister have a job?"

"She worked with me at the training center for a while as the receptionist slash part-time book-keeper, but then decided it was too hard to juggle her responsibilities there while caring for her son." Eva didn't add that Malina suffered from the same disorder she did, retinitis pigmentosa. Her sister was three years her senior and in the months before her death, Malina's eyesight had begun to rapidly deteriorate.

"I see. And how old is Mikey?"

"Three and a half." She glanced over at Finn, sensing there was more to these questions than mere curiosity. "Why do you ask?"

"No reason." Finn grinned and, ironically, the softening of his features made him all the more appealing. "Sorry I was playing twenty questions. As a cop, it's my nature to be nosy."

"Occupational hazard, huh?"

"Yep." Finn expertly navigated the busy Queens traffic as he drove to the K-9 headquarters. Eva paid attention to the streets they passed to familiarize herself with the area.

"I really appreciate you taking the time to do this, Eva."

She did her best to smile, hoping it didn't look too forced. "I want to find the man who took Cocoa as much as anyone."

"How's the cheek?"

"I'll live." Truth was, her face was tender and sore to the touch, but not bad enough that she needed medical care.

Finn drove until he found a parking spot in the tiny lot adjacent to the building. She climbed out of the white SUV while he released Abernathy from the back. With Abernathy between them, she followed him through the double glass doors that led into the main lobby area. Finn punched in the code that allowed them access so they could go inside.

A woman in uniform sat behind a large U-shaped desk wearing a headset. She appeared calm despite the never-ending ringing of the phone.

Finn waved at the officer, who handed a visitor badge to him while still talking on the phone. He clipped it to Eva's collar, then led the way inside. The interior of the police station smelled like old coffee, animal hair and the faint odor of gun oil. There were cubicles separating the desks, but she could still hear cops talking at the same time, some on the phone, some to each other. The din made it difficult to hear specific conversations, and the entire place seemed to be one of perpetual chaos.

"Is Joey Calderone around?" Finn asked the officer closest to him. "He's supposed to meet us here."

"I'm here." A man about her age came over. He also had a visitor badge clipped to his collar. "What's going on?"

"Joey, this is Eva Kendall, and she saw the man who dognapped one of Stella's puppies."

Joey, a man who was as short as he was wide, looked horrified. "That's awful. Why would anyone steal a puppy?"

"No clue, but I intend to ask when I find him." Finn's jovial tone held an underlying note of steel. "Have a seat, Eva. Joey is a master at getting sketches done from witnesses just like you. This shouldn't take too long."

Eva sat down in the uncomfortable plastic chair, thinking that Joey hadn't ever had to work with someone with such limited vision as hers. Still, she was determined to give this her best shot.

The questions started out easy, the shape of his face, his build. Eva relaxed as the drawing materialized in front of her. But when it came down to identifying details like the shape of his eyes, his nose and his mouth, helplessness washed over her.

"I'm sorry, but I don't remember." She sensed Joey's frustration, but he kept his tone light and easy.

"It's okay. Just close your eyes for a moment, see if anything comes back to you."

She closed her eyes, forcing herself to remember the brief flashes she'd got of the attacker's face. After several long moments, she opened her eyes. "I'm sorry," she repeated. "But other than a unibrow over his eyes and the five-o'clock shadow, I can't tell you anything more specific."

"That's okay. It's better to have something than nothing," Joey assured her. He put a few finishing touches on the drawing, but even she could tell the face lacked depth.

It could have been anyone. Even Joey.

"How does it look?" Finn and Abernathy crossed over to see the portrait. She imagined Finn was disappointed, but he didn't say anything. "Thanks, Joey." He took the drawing and handed it to another officer. "Calvin, I need you to spread this sketch around to the rest of the precincts, so all cops can keep an eye out for him. He's the one who stole one of Stella's puppies."

Calvin looked surprised at the directive, but then nodded. "Yeah, sure. I can do that."

Eva knew when she was being patronized and couldn't prevent a flash of anger. She jumped up from the plastic chair, grabbed her purse off the back and threw it over her shoulder. "I told you this wouldn't work. I told you I didn't get a good look at him. It wasn't well lit inside the building and everything happened so fast."

"It's okay," Finn began, but she'd had enough.

She turned quickly and made her way through the various desks of the precinct toward the door.

It wasn't until she was outside and walking away from the police station that she realized she was more upset with herself than with Finn Gallagher. She should have tried harder to get a good look at the guy. She knew the limitations of her vision but hadn't attempted to compensate for it.

Instead of trying to stop the big hulk of a man with nothing more than her keys, she should have studied his features, memorizing them for future reference.

Her shoulders slumped with defeat. It would be her fault if Cocoa was lost forever.

Finn was flabbergasted by Eva's abrupt departure. What had he said to set her off like that? He couldn't imagine. He knew civilians didn't have the same observation skills that were drilled into new recruits during their training at the academy. Having her come work with the sketch artist had been a long shot, but he'd felt it was worth it.

He hadn't expected her to become so angry and upset.

"Wow, you must be losing your touch," Joey said dryly. "What happened to the infamous Gallagher charm?"

"No clue," he admitted. He wasn't necessarily proud of his reputation with women but hadn't actively done anything to change it, either. He dated often, but never more than a few times with one woman before moving on. Despite that, he hadn't left a trail of broken hearts behind. He'd worked hard to make sure the women he went out with knew he was all about fun and nothing more serious. He had Christian values after all, so he'd never crossed the line. And they'd always parted as friends.

But Eva was different from the women he usually went out with. Not just because she was stunningly beautiful, but because of the many complex facets to her personality. Layers he was dying to peel away in order to catch a glimpse of the real woman hiding beneath.

Not that he would be getting that chance anytime soon, he thought wryly. Which was too bad, since she intrigued him in a way the others hadn't. Unfortunately, he wasn't relationship material. His dad had been a cop and his mother had left them both when he was just a kid. He remembered being huddled in his bed, listening to his parents fight. His mother had railed at his father that sitting around waiting for him to get home wasn't fair, especially when she wasn't even sure he'd come home safely. She'd screamed at him that the reality of being a cop's wife wasn't what she'd signed up for and that she was leaving.

Finn's mother had never come back.

"She's a looker. You gonna just let her leave like that?" Joey asked, breaking into his thoughts.

"No. Come, Abernathy." He followed Eva outside, figuring that once she'd got outside she'd change her mind and wait by the police-marked SUV for him to take her home.

But he was wrong. Emerging from the building, he headed toward the spot where he'd left his vehicle, then stopped when he noticed Eva wasn't waiting by the SUV. In fact, she wasn't anywhere in sight. He frowned, sweeping his gaze over the area, trying to imagine which way she'd gone. Had she called a car service?

A glimpse of golden-blond hair caught his gaze, and he was shocked to see that Eva was already several blocks away. Did she really intend to walk all the way home? Or was she heading toward the subway station?

Was she familiar with the Jackson Heights area? He wasn't sure.

Muttering under his breath, he and Abernathy picked up the pace in order to catch up with her. Not because he believed the neighborhood was dangerous, but he had promised to take her home. She'd been assaulted just a few hours earlier, and it didn't sit right to have her leaving on her own like this.

"Eva!" He called her name, hoping she'd stop and wait up for him. But the streets of New York were always packed with people and, from what he could tell, she didn't act as if she heard him.

She seemed to be heading toward one of the subway stations, so he tried to move faster, bumping into people as he attempted to navigate around them.

"Excuse me. Pardon me. Sorry," he said as he jostled the pedestrians around him. Abernathy kept up with him, as if sensing they were on the hunt. "Eva! Wait up!"

She hesitated, turning to look behind her. He waved, hoping she'd recognize him.

But she simply turned back in the direction she'd been going. He scowled, wondering if she was purposefully leading him on. He'd never chased a woman in his life and wasn't sure why on earth he was doing it now.

For some illogical reason, he didn't want her to go off alone. The dognapper was probably long gone—the perp had no reason to stick around—but Finn still didn't like it. Abernathy brushed against his legs as they attempted to close the gap between them. Eva paused at the next intersection, her gaze focused on the subway station up ahead.

"Stubborn as an ox," he said to Abernathy as

they reached the same intersection. He'd only taken two steps when he heard her shriek.

"No! Let go of me! Help! Help!"

"Eva!" Finn managed to shove past an older guy standing in front of him as he attempted to catch up to her. His gaze narrowed when he realized there was a big man tugging on her arm. Realizing the man was trying to get her into a waiting car, he yelled again. "Police! Let her go!"

Finn barreled through the crowd just as Eva was pushed backward directly toward him. He took his eyes off the assailant in time to catch her.

"It's Finn. I've got you!" He clutched Eva close to his chest, breathing hard. His heart—or maybe it was hers—thundered against his ribs. The man jumped into the car and it took off, disappearing into traffic. Finn squinted in an effort to see the license plate, but the cars were too close together. Hopefully he'd get something off one of the cameras nearby. Frustrated and worried, he turned his attention to Eva. "Are you all right?"

"I think so." Her voice was breathless, and he was grateful she made no move to push him away. He wanted—needed—to keep holding her, making sure she was truly not harmed. Abernathy sniffed at her, his tail wagging as if he was also glad she was okay.

As other subway goers brushed past them, Finn could hardly wrap his brain around what had just happened. If he hadn't been there, the big man would have succeeded in getting her into the car, abducting her.

Finally, she straightened, putting a little distance between them. "I'm okay," she said.

"That was too close," he said, more than a little upset at the attempt so close to their K-9 headquarters. He pulled out his phone. "Patricia? Tell Danielle Abbott I need to get the video feed from the cameras located near the subway station to the south of headquarters."

"Will do," the officer promised.

He turned back to Eva. "Sure you're not hurt?"

"I'm sure." She allowed him to gently tug her out of the stream of pedestrian traffic. Abernathy sat beside him, waiting for his next command. He bent to give the K-9 a quick rub, then focused on Eva.

"What happened?"

Eva lifted a trembling hand and tucked a strand of long blond hair behind her ear. "A guy came up beside me and grabbed my arm, telling me I had to go with him in the black car, a four-door sedan. I screamed for help, then I heard you call out. That's when he pushed me backward and jumped into the car to escape."

Finn nodded. Her story was exactly what he'd seen. He wanted to pull her close again but managed to refrain. He thought back, trying to put an image in his head of the man who'd been beside her. He'd seen the guy only from the back, and he was dressed from head to toe in black. There had been a tattoo of sorts peeking out from beneath the sleeve of his T-shirt. Eva hadn't mentioned a tattoo but said she'd got only a glimpse of the guy. "Did you recognize him? Was it the same man who stole Cocoa?"

There was a long pause before she finally shook her head. "You're going to think I'm nuts, but no. It wasn't the same man."

He wasn't sure he agreed but let it go for the moment. This latest attempt on Eva had to be related to the Cocoa dognapping. It was the only thing that made sense.

But how? And why?

THREE

Shaken by her second attack in less than a couple of hours, Eva longed to step into Finn's broad arms, soaking up his strength. What in the world was going on? She had no idea, other than she knew the man had almost got away with dragging her into the car. If not for her cry for help, and the way Finn had announced he was a cop and called her by name, she was certain she'd already be a hostage in the car being taken to who knows where.

She shivered, realizing how stupid she had been to leave the police station alone. Especially since her motivation was nothing more than wounded pride.

"This has to be related to the incident from this morning." Finn's voice broke into her thoughts. "And from what I could tell, the guy was dressed in black and wearing a ball cap, the same as how you described the man from this morning. If we can get the camera footage, we may catch a glimpse of his face or the license plate of the car."

"That's fine, but it wasn't the same man," she insisted, battling a wave of frustration. She tried to think of a way to make him understand. "This guy was slighter in build and sounded—different. His voice was raspy and he smelled kind of dusty."

"Raspy and dusty?" His voice held a note of skepticism. "Okay, then, did you notice anything different about the voice or scent from the guy who took Cocoa from the training center?"

"He smelled stinky, like he needed a shower, not dusty." She thought back for a moment. "And there was a twang in his voice, as if he may have been from somewhere else. A hint of the South, maybe." When Finn's eyebrows levered upward she felt defensive all over again. "Never mind. I know this may seem crazy to you as a cop, but that's the only way I can describe the difference between the two men. Thanks again for coming to my rescue."

"Hold on, Eva." Finn reached out and caught her hand. Ridiculous that she liked the feel of his warm fingers cradling hers. "I'm sorry. Sounds and smells are important, so I appreciate the extra clues. We'll get this guy, and the one who took Cocoa, too. But right now, I'm going to take you home."

The word *home* brought an image of Mikey.

Mikey! What if her presence put the child in danger? For the first time in years, she was tempted to pray, to ask God to watch over her young nephew. "Okay, but can we please hurry? I'd like to pick up my nephew from preschool. My brother-in-law is out of town for the week at a training conference in Atlanta, so I'm taking care of his son. It's a bit early to pick him up, but I'll feel better once he's with me."

"Not a problem. Let's head back to the station, where I left my SUV." Finn put his arm around her waist and, despite her determination to remain independent, she was grateful for his support. Abernathy walked along Finn's other side, and she couldn't help thinking about Cocoa.

Why had the pup been taken by the stinky Southern-twang guy? And why had the raspy-voiced man tried to drag her into the car? None of it made any sense.

Worst of all, she feared for her nephew.

"Do you think Mikey will be in danger?" she asked as they made their way toward his SUV. "Maybe I should move to a hotel temporarily."

"Where do you live?" Finn asked.

"I'm staying at my brother-in-law's for now, while I take care of Mikey. He has a small house in Forest Hills, not far from the training center."

"What about when you're not staying at Pete's place?" Finn asked. His tone was casual, but she sensed he really wanted to know.

"I rent a room in a three-bedroom house owned by one of my college roommates. Her parents are doctors at the hospital and bought it for her. The house is only about five miles from Pete's. I can walk to the training facility or take a short subway ride if the weather is bad."

"Okay, let's pick up Mikey and head back to the house. We'll figure out the next steps later." Finn steered her toward the SUV and opened the passenger door for her, then the back hatch for Abernathy.

Traffic was always a challenge, especially getting from Jackson Heights over to Forest Hills. Eva could feel her nerves fraying with every stoplight and every bumper-to-bumper slowdown. Logically she knew the two men in black had been after her and Cocoa, not Mikey, but she wouldn't rest easy until she had the little boy safe at home.

The preschool wasn't far, and when Finn pulled up beside it, she told him she'd be right back, shoved open her door and jumped out. Quickly, she went inside, then paused, waiting for her eyes to adjust from the bright sunlight to the dim interior of the building.

"Auntie Eva!" She heard Mikey before she saw him running toward her.

"Mikey!" She swept the little boy into her arms, cuddling him close. His blond hair was so much like hers that people often assumed she was the boy's mother. "I'm here to take you home."

"You're early." Peggy Harris, Mikey's pre-school teacher, came over to stand beside her. "We were in the middle of a Father's Day art project."

"I know. I'm sorry." Eva didn't want to go into the events of her morning, so she simply offered a wan smile. "Tomorrow he'll be here for the full day."

"That's fine." Peggy reached out to smooth Mikey's hair. "You can finish your art project tomorrow, Mikey. Be a good boy today for your aunt Eva, okay?"

"'Kay," Mikey said agreeably.

Eva held her nephew in her arms as she turned to head back to the doorway, assuming Finn was waiting outside in the SUV. It occurred to her that she didn't have Mikey's car seat, and the thought of walking back to Pete's house, the way she normally did, wasn't very appealing. Being outside made her feel vulnerable, and she refused to risk anything happening to Mikey.

She turned around and went back to find Peggy. "Do you have a car seat I can use temporarily?"

"Sure, you can borrow this one." She pulled a bulky car seat from the supply closet. "We have a few extras, but try to remember to bring it back as soon as you can."

"I will. Thanks, Peggy." Eva carried the car seat with one hand while holding Mikey's hand with the other.

Finn and Abernathy were coming into the building as she and Mikey came out. "Next time, wait for me," Finn chided without heat. "Parking is a nightmare around here."

"Doggy!" Mikey tugged on her hand, reaching out toward Abernathy. "I wanna pet the doggy!"

Finn laughed, a hearty sound that sent shivers of awareness down her spine. She had no idea why on earth she had this strong reaction to the sound of his laugher, but she found herself smiling as she released her nephew.

Finn crouched next to Mikey, placing his hand on Mikey's shoulder. "Friend, Abernathy," Finn said.

"Good doggy," Mikey said, stroking Abernathy's silky fur. "Nice doggy."

"His name is Abernathy," Finn explained, then cocked his head to the side. "That seems like a mouthful for such a little guy like you. Maybe you can call him Abe."

"Abe," Mikey repeated.

"And I'm Officer Finn," he added.

Abernathy attempted to lick Mikey's face, which sent the little boy into gales of laughter. Finn chuckled, and for a moment she could easily imagine the K-9 cop with a child of his own.

It was enough to snap her out of her reverie.

Having a child—a family of her own—wasn't part of her future.

Losing her eyesight would make it difficult enough to take care for herself, much less a child.

The sooner she accepted that reality, the better.

Finn loved watching Mikey and Abernathy together. Boys and dogs went together like peanut butter and jelly. But it was time to get going, so he called Abernathy over.

"Come," he commanded.

Abernathy instantly wheeled around and came to sit beside Finn, looking up at him expectantly. "Time to go." He led the way down the street to the parking spot he'd managed to find. When they reached the vehicle, he opened the back. Abernathy jumped inside with lithe grace.

Finn came around to help Eva with the car seat. Once she had it secure, she set Mikey inside, buckling him in. He opened the front passenger-side door for her, and she hesitated for a moment before climbing in.

After sliding in behind the wheel, Finn glanced over at her. "I was thinking once you're safe at home, I could go out and grab something for lunch."

She hesitated, then nodded, seemingly relived. "That would be great. I'm still too shaken up to cook."

"Any particular food Mikey likes best?" NYC

was well-known for its variety of restaurants, but he had no clue what three-year-old kids preferred to eat.

"Pizza!" Mikey said excitedly. "I love pizza!"

"I know you do," Eva said, glancing back at her nephew. "It's your favorite, right? We'll eat as soon as we're home."

"Speaking of which, I'll need directions."

"Keep heading north, then turn left at the next intersection."

Eva continued to give him directions until he pulled into a narrow driveway in front of an older-model brown brick home wedged in between two others. It was a nice place to raise a child, he thought as he slid the gearshift into Park. He thought there might even be a little sliver of a fenced-in backyard for Mikey to play in.

"We're home," Eva said, as she carried Mikey out of the SUV. Finn went around to the back to let Abernathy out, grabbing the dog's water dish and tucking it under his arm as he followed Eva and Mikey inside.

Eva hesitated for a moment in the doorway, and he wondered if she'd noticed something out of place. "What's wrong?"

"Oh, nothing." She flushed as if she were embarrassed, then moved farther inside. The small kitchen was crowded with two adults, a little boy and a dog, but Eva acted as if she didn't notice.

"Okay, what's for lunch?" he asked, filling Abernathy's water dish and setting it in the corner of the kitchen.

"Ordering pepperoni pizza would be easiest, then you don't have to leave." There was an underlying note of fear in Eva's voice and he understood she was loath to be alone.

"Not a problem." He caught a glimpse of a local pizza flyer on the fridge. Using his cell, he dialed the number and ordered a cheese-and-pepperoni pizza. When that was done, he took Abernathy's vest off, giving him a bit of freedom to explore. Abernathy lapped at the water, then began sniffing around the edges of the room.

Finn's phone rang and he quickly answered it. "Gallagher."

"We got the video feed you requested," Danielle Abbott, their technical guru said. "But it's not a lot of help. The camera angle isn't great. The cars are too close together to get a view of the license plate, and the crowds of people on the sidewalk obscure the view of the perp's face. I'll keep trying to clear up the video, but I can't make any promises."

Finn battled a wave of frustration. "Okay. Thanks, Danielle."

"What?" Eva asked.

"We haven't got anything off the subway camera. At least, not yet."

Eva shook her head. "It figures."

The pizza arrived twenty minutes later. Eva

opened her purse, but he shooed her away to take care of the bill himself. Eva set the table, and he opened the pizza box, then picked up Mikey to place him in his booster seat. Eva took out a small slice of pizza and placed it on Mikey's plate, giving it a chance to cool off. He took the seat across from Eva's and, when she finished, he clasped his hands together and bowed his head to say grace.

"Dear Lord, we thank You for this food we are about to eat. We also thank You for keeping Eva safe in Your care. Please provide us the wisdom and guidance to find Cocoa, too. Amen."

There was a brief pause before Eva murmured, "Amen."

Mikey had already taken a bite of pizza, completely oblivious to the prayer. Finn smiled and made a mental note to include the boy next time.

Whoa, wait a minute. Next time? There wasn't going to be a next time! He was only here because Eva had been attacked twice in one day.

This might look like a nice cozy scene, but Eva wasn't his woman and Mikey wasn't his son.

"Finn?"

He looked up from his food, belatedly realizing he was staring at it without making the slightest effort to eat. "What is it?"

"Do you think we'll be okay here?"

"I think so, yes." He picked up a slice of pizza and took a bite, chewing thoughtfully. He didn't want to say too much in front of the boy. "It's probably better for you to be here than at your own place."

She nodded thoughtfully. "I hope so."

"How many people know that your brother-in-law is out of town?"

"My roommates know, of course. So does my boss." She nibbled at her pizza.

"How long will he be gone?"

"About six more days, he left yesterday. He's a paramedic and firefighter, stationed not far from Mercy Medical Center here in Queens. He's their trainer, and there's some new strategies about caring for patients in the field he has to learn, so they sent him to Atlanta." She was silent for a moment before adding, "It wasn't easy for him to leave so soon after…" Her voice trailed off.

Finn nodded his understanding. He couldn't imagine losing your wife and then leaving your son behind as you went off on a business trip. "It's great that you're able to be here for Mikey."

"Yes." Her smile held a hint of sadness. "Between the two of us, we'll help him through this."

It was on the tip of his tongue to ask about God and faith, but then remembered how she hadn't immediately joined him in saying grace. Maybe that was part of his role here. Not just to protect her, but to help Eva understand God's grace and the power of prayer.

Mikey played with his food, pretending his slice of pizza was a plane and dive-bombing his silverware. Crumbs from the pizza crust were falling everywhere, and he noticed that Abernathy had taken up residence next to Mikey's chair, gobbling up every morsel the kid dropped.

Finn tried not to wince. Normally Abernathy wouldn't eat from anyone other than him, but with his vest off, he obviously thought Mikey's crumbs were fair game.

"Don't play with your food," Eva said, putting her hand on Mikey's arm. "Are you full? Or do you want to eat some more?"

"Eat," Mikey said, popping what was left of his pizza into his mouth. "Can I visit Cocoa?"

Eva froze, her gaze locking onto his. She drew in a shaky breath, then told the little boy the truth, "I'm sorry to say Cocoa is lost, Mikey, so you can't visit now. But Officer Finn is going to work really hard to find him."

"Yes, I will." Finn wasn't exactly sure how he would accomplish that feat since he didn't have a clue where to start. Earlier, he'd taken Eva's keys with him back to the station and had asked Ilona, the lab tech, to run the DNA. Once those results came back, they'd know if the perp who'd hit Eva was in the system or not. But how long would that take? Despite what was portrayed on TV, fast turnaround times for DNA happened only in rare circumstances. A puppy-napping wouldn't be high on the list.

"I'm sorry about what happened this morning," he said. He couldn't imagine what he'd do if someone took Abernathy from him. The dog was more than just his partner.

Abernathy was the only family Finn had since his father had passed away last year. The other K-9 officers were like his brothers, but Abernathy was more than that. The K-9 was his best friend.

"I know." She offered a lopsided smile. He knew she was worried about more than just Cocoa's fate.

"I'll take a look around the place when we're finished," Finn offered. "See if there are any extra security measures I can add."

"I'd appreciate that," Eva said gratefully. "I know we're probably fine here, but I don't want to take any chances."

He wanted to offer to stay there with her but knew he shouldn't get too emotionally involved. Bad enough that he was tempted to ask her out for dinner and maybe a movie. What was it about her that made him want to toss his two-date, nothing-serious dating rules out the window?

Five minutes later it was clear Mikey was finished eating. Eva washed tomato sauce off his face and his hands, then lifted him down to the floor. Finn finished his meal so he could help clean up.

"I'll take care of it," she said, shooing him away with a wave of her hand. "Do me a favor and check things out, would you? I know I'm being paranoid, but I want to be sure we're safe."

"No problem." Finn moved through the house, taking note of the layout. A living room was located through the doorway from the kitchen, along with a small bathroom and a bedroom. From what he could tell, the bedroom was used as a playroom, toys strewed everywhere.

There were steps leading up to the second floor, where he surmised the other bedrooms were located.

Sure enough, he found two bedrooms separated by a full bathroom. The master suite didn't look frilly, and he wondered if Pete had already got rid of things that reminded him of his dead wife. Crossing the room, he looked out the window. Just as he'd suspected, there was a narrow fenced-in area containing a patio in which a turtle-shaped sandbox was located. There was a grill out there, too, perfect for spending summer evenings outside.

He did the same routine in Mikey's room. A look out the window revealed a wooden trellis from beneath his window to the ground. The window had a sturdy lock, but he wondered if there was something more he could do to prevent anyone from using the trellis to gain access inside. It might not hold a man's weight, but he didn't want to take any chances.

Finn made his way back downstairs to the

main level. He found Mikey in the playroom. Abernathy was stretched out on the floor, his tail thumping against the linoleum.

Eva joined him a few minutes later. "Any thoughts?"

Finn glanced at her. "Just the trellis against the wall outside Mikey's window." He kept his voice low so the little boy wouldn't overhear.

Her blue eyes clouded with fear. "Maybe I'll have him sleep in the master suite for the rest of the week."

"Not a bad idea," he agreed. "I'll call the 110th Precinct and ask for cops to drive by on a regular basis."

"That would be nice." Once again her smile was sad, and Finn found himself wishing there was a way he could lighten the burden she seemed to be carrying around with her.

"Auntie Eva, look!" Mikey picked up the small furry stuffed replica of Cocoa she'd given to him the day she started working with the puppy. "Here's my Cocoa. I wanna play with your Cocoa."

Finn knew that a missing puppy was a difficult concept for a three-year-old boy to understand, and Eva glanced at him as if she wasn't sure how much to tell her nephew.

Since he was hardly an expert on little kids, he had no clue, either.

"I already told you, sweetie, Cocoa is missing,"

Eva said gently. "He's lost, but Officer Finn and Abernathy here are going to find him."

Mikey's expression clouded, and Finn was afraid the little boy was about to burst into tears. "Maybe the bad man has him."

What? Finn glanced at Eva, wondering if he'd heard the child correctly.

Eva had gone pale. She dropped to her knees beside Mikey so she could look him in the eye. "What bad man, sweetie? Did you see a bad man?"

Mikey dropped his stuffed Cocoa and picked up two plastic dinosaurs, slamming them together with glee.

"What do you think?" Finn asked in a soft voice. "Do you think he saw something?"

"I don't know." Eva's expression was full of concern. "He's only three years old. Maybe he just heard something on TV."

"He watches cop shows?" Finn asked wryly.

"No, but have you seen some of the cartoons? Several have bad guys in them."

"Bad guy," Mikey repeated. "Mommy said the bad guy is real, not make-believe."

"Mommy said that?" Eva asked in horror. She swayed as if she might go down, so Finn put his arm around her waist.

"Easy," he murmured near her ear. "If Mikey sees that you're upset, he'll cry."

"I don't understand," she whispered. "What

does he mean? Why would Malina tell him the bad man is real?"

Finn had no clue, but he remembered seeing her sister's name on the list of people who had been fired from the training center. Something Eva didn't seem to know.

He wondered if there had been more going on in Malina's life than Eva was aware of.

FOUR

Eva pulled herself together with an effort. She sat down on the floor next to Mikey and picked up one of his dinosaurs before casually asking, "Do you remember when Mommy talked about the bad man?"

Mikey shook his head and picked up the T. rex, his favorite dinosaur, and began making growling noises. "Grr! I'm gonna eat you for breakfast."

"No, don't eat me!" Eva cried as she pranced her dinosaur away as if trying to escape. "My dinosaur is scared of the T. rex. Mikey, was your mommy scared of the bad man?"

This time, Mikey nodded. "Bad mans are scary. But my T. rex is scarier." He went back to making growling noises.

Eva glanced up at Finn, who was watching their interaction with a thoughtful expression on his face. While playing with the dinosaurs, she tried several times to probe about her sister's bad man, but Mikey was too focused on the dinosaurs and didn't provide any additional information.

Giving up, she set down her stegosaurus and began to stand. Finn was there, offering his hand. She took it and allowed him to help her up, keenly aware of the warmth of his fingers cradling hers. "Thanks," she said, releasing his hand while hoping her cheeks weren't as pink from embarrassment as they felt.

Finn lifted his chin toward the kitchen. "I need to talk to you for a moment about Malina." He glanced down at his K-9 partner. "Abernathy, stay and guard."

The yellow Lab instantly sat and lowered his nose toward Mikey. The little boy laughed and abandoned his dinosaurs to give the Lab a hug. "I love Abe," he said, his voice muffled against the dog's fur.

"Me, too," Finn agreed with a smile.

Eva moved into the kitchen area. When they were out of earshot of the little boy, she glanced at Finn quizzically. "What about Malina?"

He hesitated, then asked, "Why did she leave the guide dog training center?"

"Because she was finding it difficult to keep working as the receptionist there while taking care of Mikey."

"Isn't Mikey in preschool?"

"Yes, but Pete's schedule requires him to work twenty-four hours on and then he gets forty-eight hours off. The calls come in all night long when he's on duty, so he rarely gets any sleep. Once he gets home, he heads straight to bed. By the time he's on a normal sleep schedule, he ends up going back in for another shift." She shrugged. "I think Pete's long hours were getting to her, so she decided to quit."

"Is that what Wade Yost told you?"

"No, that's what Malina told me." She frowned, not appreciating Finn's skeptical tone. "Why? What difference does it make why Malina left the training center?"

"It doesn't," Finn said, averting his gaze. "I just think it's an odd coincidence. Less than a month after she quits her job, she's hit by a car and Mikey is talking about some sort of bad man. I'm just trying to understand how the puzzle pieces fit together."

Eva folded her arms over her chest. "You're making a bigger deal out of this than there is. Mikey has been through a lot, losing his mother and adjusting to life without her. How do we know he isn't just a bit confused? Maybe heard something on television? I'm not sure we should jump into action based on a three-year-old's statement."

"You're probably right." Again his tone lacked conviction. "Still, do you know if she had any enemies? Or if Pete has any? Any issues at all?"

Eva let out a heavy sigh. "None that I know of.

Why would they? They were happily married and both doted on Mikey. I just don't see how they could be involved with some sort of bad man."

"Was her death investigated?"

"Yes, but it was deemed a hit-and-run, and there wasn't reason to think she was purposely hit. No one nearby got the license plate or paid any attention to the driver." She thought back to those turbulent and sorrowful days after Malina's accident. "The police didn't have any leads and told us that unless someone stepped forward with more information, they likely wouldn't find the person responsible."

"That must have been difficult for you to hear," Finn said. His green eyes were so intense she found it impossible to look away.

"It was," she admitted. "I'm sure the driver was texting behind the wheel, since a few witnesses mentioned noticing erratic driving. To think that a text message cost my sister her life makes me so mad."

Finn nodded but didn't ask anything further. Eva's initial annoyance faded as she looked at Finn. Dressed in his uniform, he was handsome enough to make her wish for a cure for her retinitis pigmentosa.

But that was akin to longing for the end to world hunger, so she did her best to pull her gaze away. Finn was good-looking enough to have any woman he wanted. He wouldn't be interested in a woman who would be declared legally blind in a few years.

"Listen, I need to get back to headquarters. I still have paperwork to write up about Cocoa's kidnapping and the attempt on you. Is there anything else you need before I go?"

The thought of him leaving brought a flash of panic, but she did her best not to show it. Remembering the hard grasp of the raspy guy's fingers against her arm made her shiver despite the warmth. She forced a casual smile. "Um, no, I don't think so. Thanks for lunch and, well, for everything you've done for us."

"You're welcome." Finn stared at her for a moment, then reached for his phone. "Do you mind taking down my personal cell number? I'd like yours, too. You know, in case we find someone who matches the sketch."

Eva wasn't holding out much hope for the sketch but readily agreed to take Finn's number. "Of course."

They exchanged cell numbers quickly, then Finn called Abernathy over. "Eva, don't hesitate to call if you need something, okay?"

"I won't. Oh, I need to get Mikey's car seat out of your SUV."

"Leave it," Finn said. "What time do you work in the morning? I'll stop by and pick you and Mikey up, so you don't have to walk or use the subway."

His offer was sweet. "Are you sure? I hate to take you out of your way."

"I'm sure."

"Okay, then. I usually try to get to work by seven thirty in the morning. The preschool opens at seven."

"I'll meet you here at seven, then. That way you'll still get to work on time."

She nodded and watched as Finn took Abernathy outside and put him in the back of the SUV. After sliding behind the wheel, he backed out of the driveway and was gone before she could think of an excuse that would allow him to stay.

Reminding herself of her goal to remain independent, Eva locked the door and returned to the playroom to spend time with Mikey.

But as the hours dragged by, she found it impossible to concentrate. She made spaghetti for dinner and then gave Mikey his bath before tucking him into Pete's bed, using the master suite because she was leery of the trellis.

Too wired to sleep, Eva moved through the rest of the house, going from window to window, peering into the darkness to make sure no one was out there. A mostly futile effort, since her eyesight was especially limited in the darkness.

People walked briskly along the sidewalks, and she did her best to catch a glimpse of them as they moved beneath the streetlight. From what

she could tell, there was no sign of the stinky guy
or raspy guy anywhere.

But the two men followed her into her dreams,
turning them into nightmares, and her throat was
raw from her silent screams.

At headquarters, Finn finished up his paperwork, then quickly performed a background
check on Malina Kendall-Stallings to see if there
could be any possible link between the attempts
on Eva and the dead woman. He came up empty.
Eva's older sister had a clean record.

He squelched a flash of guilt for thinking the
worst about her. As a cop, he wouldn't be doing
his job if he didn't follow up on every possible
lead. Yet he could understand why Eva had got
upset with him. Her sister had been the innocent
victim of a tragic hit-and-run accident. From the
110th Precinct officers, he'd easily validated that
there had been no indication of foul play.

So what if she'd been fired from the guide dog
training center? That didn't mean she was involved in anything criminal. He needed to stay
focused on finding Cocoa and the men responsible for the assaults against Eva.

Less than an hour later, he and Abernathy were
called out for a missing ten-year-old child. Lilliana Chow was late getting home from school, and
her mother was desperately worried. Finn didn't

hesitate to take Abernathy with him to head over to the Lindenwood area of Queens.

By the time he fought the never-ending traffic to get there, the little girl had returned home. According to her mother, Lilliana had missed her subway stop and, rather than taking the subway back, had decided to walk.

Finn was glad his and Abernathy's services weren't needed and, since he was in the area, decided to take a drive, see if he could find any clues related to the two men who'd attacked Eva.

It was crazy to think he'd be able to pick up the raspy guy from the rather generic sketch that Eva had produced, but it was better than dwelling on the loss of his chief, Jordan Jameson, who'd been found dead with a needle mark in his arm. At first the rumor was suicide, but Finn and the rest of the NYC K-9 Command Unit knew their chief had been murdered. They continued to work together in an effort to crack the case, but the longer it took, the more likely it was that the perp would get away with the crime. A confusing part of the crime was that Jordan's K-9 partner, a German shepherd named Snapper, had been missing since Jordan's death.

The K-9 should have stayed with the fallen officer as he was trained to do. Finn had thought Snapper must have been stolen, but there was a recent report of a male German shepherd on the loose in a Queens park, and everyone was looking for him. Had Snapper been stolen and escaped? Finn had no idea, but he couldn't help wondering if the stolen puppy was related to Jordan's missing K-9.

Finn returned to headquarters and viewed the subway video for himself, frustrated by the lack of information to be gleaned from the limited view of the street where Eva had been accosted. With few clues to go on, Finn finished his shift and decided to head back toward Forest Hills, telling himself that driving past Pete's house was on the way home. He lived in Briarwood, in the same house where he'd grown up with his father. His dad had passed away last year from a sudden heart attack. At the time, Finn had half expected his mother to show up to claim her portion of the property, but she never did.

The house was too big for a single guy, but there was a small yard that was good for Abernathy so Finn had decided to stay. He was slowly renovating the place, putting money into updating the bathrooms and, ultimately, the kitchen, with thoughts of one day putting it on the market.

Although he wasn't sure he was ready to leave his childhood memories behind. Looking back, the good memories outweighed the bad.

Driving slowly past Pete Stalling's house, he searched for any indication that someone was watching the place. He went around the block twice before he was convinced no one was lurking around.

It was tempting to pull into the driveway, to check in on Eva and Mikey, but he told himself to keep going. It wasn't like him to get hung up on a woman, and he was irritated with himself that he hadn't been able to get Eva out of his mind.

She wasn't like the other women he dated for fun and laughs. She was serious and intense. Stubborn and smart. Courageous and gentle. And so beautiful she took his breath away.

All very good reasons to keep their relationship professional and friendly.

No matter how much he secretly wished for something more.

The next morning, Eva took Mikey through the routine of getting dressed and his teeth brushed before heading down to the kitchen to make breakfast. Yawning, she made a half pot of coffee. She'd been awake more than she'd slept, thanks to the troubling nightmares, which didn't bode well for the rest of her day.

When she spilled coffee down her yellow knit top, she headed back upstairs to change. It wasn't as if she needed fancy clothes working with dogs all day, but she still wanted to look nice. For Finn? Maybe. As she rifled through the items in her small suitcase, she realized she'd underestimated how many times she'd have to change clothes because of being around a three-year-old. Mikey had got jelly smears over one top already the previous day, then there had been the tomato sauce handprint from the spaghetti dinner last night and now the coffee spill. She could do laundry but didn't have enough yet for a load, so she made a mental note to stop by her place to grab more clothing before picking up Mikey from preschool.

Returning to the kitchen, this time wearing a burnt-orange short-sleeved blouse with her jeans, she made Mikey breakfast. Her nephew loved pancakes, so she whipped up a batch, making half a dozen for them to share. As she set his plate before him and dropped into the seat beside him, she was reminded of how Finn had said grace the day before. It had felt a little awkward watching him pray, yet, at the same time, she was touched by his faith.

She and Malina had been raised to believe in God, but their parents hadn't attended church on a regular basis and had never prayed before every meal. The little childhood customs had gone away after her mother lost her eyesight, the same way Eva was destined to do. Her parents now lived in Arizona, and she only saw them a few times a year.

After learning about her diagnosis and Malina's untimely death, she'd begun to doubt that God existed.

"More syrup," Mikey said, breaking into her thoughts.

"How do you ask nicely?" She reached for the bottle of maple syrup but didn't pour any onto his pancakes until Mikey responded.

"Please," Mikey said, stretching for the bottle.

"I'll help you." She poured a generous dollop of syrup on his pancakes.

It was at times like this when she struggled the most with her diagnosis. As much as she tried to fight against the bouts of self-pity, the feelings remained buried just below the surface, ready to pop out at the least provocation.

A knock at the door made her heart jump crazily in her chest. Shaking her head at her foolishness, Eva peered through the window to see Finn and Abernathy standing there, and she unlocked the door.

"Hey." Finn greeted her with a broad smile. "I'm a little early. For some reason traffic wasn't as bad as usual."

"That's fine, come on in." She opened the door wider, giving them room to enter. "We're eating breakfast. There might be an extra pancake or two if you're hungry."

"I already ate, but I wouldn't say no to a cup of coffee."

She laughed at the hopeful expression on his face. "Of course, there's plenty."

"Hi, Officer Finn," Mikey said, waving his fork. The little boy peered down from his perch at the table. "Did you bring Abe?"

"Sure did." Finn gestured to the boy and Abernathy eagerly gave him sloppy kisses. Or maybe, Eva thought, he was simply licking the sticky syrup off him.

"Thanks," Finn said when she handed him a mug filled with coffee, then returned to finish her pancakes.

"No news on yesterday's events?" She studiously avoided using Cocoa's name, so Mikey wouldn't ask once again what happened to the puppy.

"I'm afraid not." Finn's smile faded. "But don't worry. We're keeping an eye on things."

Fifteen minutes later, using Mikey's car seat so they could return the borrowed one, they arrived at the preschool. Peggy was grateful to have the car seat back, and Mikey waved happily before running over to play with the others.

After ten minutes, they were on their way to the training center.

"I'll come inside with you," Finn said. "I need to pick up the video your boss promised me anyway."

She nodded and led the way inside the center. Finn and Abernathy followed close behind.

"Wade? Officer Gallagher is here."

Her boss came out of his office with a harried expression on his face. "Did you find Cocoa?"

"Not yet, but I'd like to view the video you have from over the past week or so, if you don't mind."

"Oh, yeah, almost forgot." Wade disappeared into his office, returning a few minutes later with a disk. "Here you go."

"Thanks." Finn took the disk and glanced at her. "I'll see you later. Stay safe, Eva, okay? And call if you need anything."

"I will." She quickly turned and went to the kennel to begin training another puppy, a black Lab named George. George was a week younger than Cocoa, and needed more work than Cocoa had. Young puppies were left at the training center until they were twelve weeks old, then were fostered out with a trainer for a full year. After the first year, the dog would be paired with an owner, and the training continued at the center until both trainer and owner were adjusted to each other.

She couldn't help wondering why Cocoa had been targeted instead of George or any of the other dogs. They had several that were about to be paired with their future owners, which made them more valuable than a young pup.

The rest of her day went by without any issues. She even went across the street to a little bodega for lunch. At two thirty in the afternoon, she went to find her boss.

"I need to leave a little early today."

"Uh?" He looked distracted, and it occurred to her that he'd made it in earlier than she had, which was highly unusual. "Oh, sure, that's fine."

"Thanks." She turned to leave, then glanced back at him. "Is something bothering you?"

He looked startled but then waved a hand. "No. I mean, other than Cocoa being gone. I've been fielding phone calls about it all day."

"Sorry to hear that." She sensed there was more going on than he was telling her but let it go. She was a trainer and preferred working with the dogs rather than the business side of things. Malina hadn't been as much of a dog lover but had enjoyed doing the books. Malina had talked about going back to school to take bookkeeping classes, but after learning about her diagnosis, she'd abandoned that dream.

Now her sister was gone.

Eva shook off the painful memories. "Bye, Wade. See you tomorrow."

"Uh-huh." Wade was already back at work, shuffling papers.

Heading into the sunshine, Eva decided to walk home. She'd been thrilled when Alecia had invited her to move into her new place, as the location was close to her work. It also wasn't far from Mercy Medical Center, where Alecia and Julie worked as nurses. Her thoughts returned to Finn, and she wondered what he was doing today, then chastised herself for caring. If he had news about Cocoa or the two men who'd assaulted her, he'd tell her. No sense making up excuses to call him.

The home she shared with her roommates was a narrow two-story building. Feeling safe in the bright daylight, she went up to the front door and used her key to unlock it. Eva had dropped out of nursing school when her sister had been diagnosed, fearing she had the same genetic disorder. And she was right. She'd switched to training guide dogs and loved it. Thankfully, she had a knack with puppies and it was something she might be able to do years from now, even after losing her eyesight.

Currently, Eva had trouble seeing at night and in dim lighting and had already noticed some limitations in her peripheral vision. As the months went on, she knew the loss of peripheral vision would continue to grow more and more noticeable until she could only see straight ahead through a round circle. Eventually the circle would narrow to a pinpoint where she might only be able to see light and dark.

Her eye doctor told her there was a potential treatment that could slow the vision loss but couldn't cure it completely. She had to go back to see him in another month to find out if she'd qualify.

"Hey, Eva, what are you doing here?" Alecia looked surprised when Eva entered the kitchen. "I thought you were staying at your brother-in-law's for the week, taking care of your nephew?"

"I am, but I need more clothes." She eyed Alecia's scrubs and then glanced at her watch. "I was expecting you to be at work."

"I'm on my way, running late as usual." Alecia rolled her eyes and sighed. "I think my boss is getting tired of me, but we're so short staffed she always ends up letting me off the hook."

Eva smiled, knowing Alecia's tardiness all too well. She and Julie had waited many times for Alecia to show when they'd made plans. "Don't let me keep you," she said, heading over to the stairs leading up to her second-floor bedroom. "I'll only be here a few minutes anyway."

"Okay, see you!" Alecia picked up her stethoscope and dashed out the door.

Eva went to her closet, pulled out a small bag and began packing a few more items, especially tops. Hopefully by the weekend, she'd get some laundry done.

A sudden crash echoed through the room, followed by a distinct thud. Her heart thumped wildly as she instinctively ducked down beside the bed. What was that? A gunshot? She pulled out her phone, intending to dial 911 when she noticed the large object sitting in the center of her hardwood floor, between the window and the bed.

What in the world? Crawling on her hands and knees, she peered closer at what she could now see was a large rock with paper wrapped around it.

Her mouth went dry as she recognized the picture of Cocoa on the paper with a crude threat written beneath.

"If you want to see the dog alive, find the package your sister stole from us."

Her sister? A package? Eva's thoughts whirled as she called Finn's cell number to report what had happened, unable to deny Cocoa's disappearance was linked in some way to Malina.

FIVE

Finn pulled up in front of Eva's place ten minutes after her call. It had helped that he'd already been on his way back to the training center to talk to her about the video. There was a brief image of a man lurking near the edge of camera range, and he hoped she might be able to identify the guy as one of the attackers.

He let Abernathy out of the SUV and took the K-9 with him as he quickly headed inside the house. He'd barely knocked at the door when it swung open. Eva stood there, trembling, so he stepped forward and wrapped his arms around her.

"Oh, Finn, it's awful." Her voice was muffled against his chest and her tear-streaked cheeks tugged at his heart. "Thankfully, my two roommates were gone when this happened, but Alecia had left barely five minutes before the incident. What if one of them had been hurt?"

"It's okay, you're safe now." She felt good in

his arms, and he wanted to continue holding her and offering comfort but needed to focus on this most recent threat. "Ready to show me the crime scene?" Eva had been so upset when she'd called that he'd had trouble understanding what she meant about a rock and a threat against Cocoa.

She pulled away from him, subtly swiping at the dampness on her face. "Yes. It happened in my room."

Finn followed her up the stairs to her second-floor bedroom, decorated with cheerful yellow paint on the walls and frilly white curtains. His gaze zeroed in on the broken window, and then at the rock on the floor surrounded by bits of broken glass.

"Stay back," he warned. "Abernathy, sit."

The yellow Lab sat beside Eva as if guarding her. Finn didn't want his K-9 to walk over the shards of glass glittering on the hardwood floor.

He pulled a large evidence bag from his pocket and picked up the rock carefully, noticing it was big and heavy enough to leave a dent in the hard-wood floor. He wrapped the edges of the bag around it to preserve it. There was a chance he'd be able to lift fingerprints, either from the rock or the paper itself.

Examining it further through the clear plastic evidence bag, he could see what Eva had meant by a threat against Cocoa. The note beneath the dog's picture said clearly that if she wanted to see the dog alive, she needed to find the package her sister had stolen.

Stepping carefully around the broken glass, he approached the shattered window. It faced the tiny backyard, which wasn't fenced in. It was empty now except for two garbage cans, one tipped over on its side. He could easily imagine someone throwing the rock from there. Eva's room was on the second floor, so not too high. The bigger question was how the perp had identified Eva's window. Being followed to the house was one thing, but knowing the specific window that belonged to her bedroom rather than her roommates? That was something different.

Or had it simply been a coincidence?

Most cops didn't believe in coincidences, and Finn was no exception. Sure, they happened on occasion but not often.

His instincts had been right all along. Whatever Malina had got involved with before her death had caused Cocoa's dognapping and three assaults—if you counted the rock incident—against Eva.

He backed away from the window and turned to look at her. "Do you have any idea what package they're talking about?"

She shook her head vehemently. "No! Absolutely not."

Her response was exactly what he'd expected, but this time he wasn't going to let it go. "I need you to think back to the time before Malina's death. Did you ever see her with a package? Did she carry a large purse? Or did you sense something was amiss?"

"No!" She lifted a shaky hand and pushed her hair behind her ear. Again he had the crazy urge to pull her into his arms to comfort her. "She had a medium-sized purse, not a large bag. I promise, Finn, I'm not lying about this. I want Cocoa back just as much as you do. If I knew anything I'd tell you."

"What about money?" Finn asked, stepping closer. "Did she seem to have enough? Or was she always broke?"

"I never had the impression she was broke or had more money than she should." He could sense the frustration in her tone but ignored it.

"Eva, I have to ask. Is there any way your sister could have been involved in something illegal?"

"No. Absolutely not." Her instant denial seemed to come from loyalty rather than certainty.

"I need you to think carefully about this," he pressed. "Cocoa's life depends on it."

She met his gaze head-on. "I know what you're thinking. Drugs, right? What else could be in a missing package?"

"Drugs, stolen goods such as precious gems or cash itself," Finn pointed out. "But yeah, those are the three main possibilities floating through my mind at the moment."

Eva shook her head. "I just can't imagine Malina being involved in anything like that. It's surreal. She had a loving husband and a beautiful son. I can't believe she'd risk her family for something like that."

"Yet the two men who assaulted you obviously believe that you know something about their stolen package."

She fell silent for a long moment. "I know. But she may have got the package by accident. Like they think she stole it, but someone set her up."

He levered one eyebrow skeptically. "Doubtful."

"But possible. I'll search my brother-in-law's house, see if I can find anything."

"Good plan. I'll help." Finn glanced back at the window. "It's interesting that the vandal knew which window to target. Are you sure you haven't noticed anyone lurking around outside? Not just today but over the past few weeks?"

"I'm positive." Again there was no hesitation in her tone. "You know as well as I do that there are always people coming and going. I had no reason to believe I was being watched, no reason to notice anyone in particular behind me." Her expression turned grim. "But you're right about the window. It freaks me out that they know so much about me. I guess I've been a bit clueless, huh?"

"Hey, it's okay." Finn reached over and took

her hand in his, giving it a reassuring squeeze. "We'll figure it out."

"I hope so." Her crystal-blue eyes were troubled. "I can't bear the thought of anything happening to Cocoa. And what about my roommates, Alecia and Julie? I hate to think they may be in danger."

Finn didn't much like it, either. "You'll have to warn them, encourage them to stay someplace else for a few days."

"I will."

It was clear to him that the perps had decided to use the dog as leverage against Eva as a way to get their precious package back. What if they weren't able to find it? If the package contained drugs, and if Malina was a user, it was highly likely the package no longer existed.

Except…he kept coming back to the hit-and-run that had taken Malina's life. What if the accident that had turned deadly had been intended as more of a scare tactic? A way to get her to turn over the stolen goods? He imagined the driver could have been a bit overzealous in an attempt to appear to be a distracted driver, hitting Malina with more force than was necessary.

The end result had been that she'd died, making it impossible for the perps to get the location of the missing package.

Warming to his theory, he decided to go back to recanvass the area around Malina's accident to see if he could resurrect any witnesses the original officers might have missed.

First, though, he needed to get this rock logged into evidence. Fingerprints would go a long way in helping them identify the perps and what they might be involved in. And he wanted to stop by the training center again to talk to Yost. He'd fired Malina for a reason and Finn wanted to know the details.

"I have a few stops to make, and then we can pick up Mikey from preschool and I'll take you home." Finn turned, hesitated and glanced back at her. "Do you have anything in the basement that I can use to board up the window?"

She nodded. "I think there are some odds and ends down there. The previous owners had done some renovation work."

"Good." He hurried to the basement and found a board large enough to nail over the broken window. When he finished the task, he made a call to Wade Yost.

"I need a few minutes of your time," he told the manager of the guide dog training center. "I need to ask you about Malina."

"Okay, but not in front of Eva."

Finn glanced at Eva, who was scratching Abernathy behind the ears. "She already knows something is up with her sister," he told Yost. "I don't think you need to worry."

"I can't afford to lose her as a trainer," Yost argued. "She's the best I have."

"I understand, but you need to trust me on this. We'll be there in a few minutes."

"Fine," Yost agreed in a resigned tone.

"Don't forget I have to pick up Mikey by five thirty," she reminded him.

He nodded. "Okay."

Eva was quiet as he drove to the training center and Finn knew she was likely thinking about her sister and the missing package. He hoped he wasn't making a mistake including her in the conversation with her boss, but he needed Eva to think hard about what her sister might have been up to.

Wade looked distinctly uncomfortable when they walked into his office, as if he was dreading what was to come. "Hey."

Finn greeted him with a nod. "We have reason to believe that Cocoa was taken by someone Malina was acquainted with." He was being vague on purpose, not wanting to give too much away. "I need to understand what happened before she left your employment."

"Uh, sure." Yost cast a furtive glance at Eva. "Uh, Malina worked as a receptionist and also did some of the bookkeeping for me. But I, uh, noticed she'd made several mistakes and that her behavior had grown erratic. She was late or left early or didn't show up at all."

"For how long?" Finn asked.

The manager shrugged. "A couple of months." Yost glanced at Eva, his gaze pleading. "Please don't be upset with me, Eva. I'm really sorry—I had no choice but to let her go."

Eva sucked in a harsh breath. "You fired her?"

"I had to!" Yost looked distressed. "I didn't want to because I respect you so much. But Malina changed. She messed up my bills, caused me to be overdrawn at the bank. I was getting pressure from the owner to take control of the finances or I'd be fired. I needed to do something, so I let her go and took over doing the books and being the receptionist myself. Please, don't quit. I need you."

Eva didn't say anything, but he knew she wasn't happy about what she'd learned.

Finn put a reassuring hand on Eva's arm. "Don't take this out on him. It's not Wade's fault." He kept his tone soft and soothing. "He cares about you. And Malina, too. But your sister must have got herself in trouble, doing something she shouldn't have been."

Eva bit her lip, her eyes filling with tears. As if sensing her distress, Abernathy nudged her with his nose. "I don't blame you, Wade, but I wish you'd confided in me! Maybe I could have done something to help her."

Understanding she had a right to be upset yet doubting that there was much Eva could have done to rescue her sister, Finn kept his hand on her arm. "And Malina could have come to you, too."

Eva didn't have a response to that.

Finn glanced back at Yost. "Anything else? Did she have her own office?"

"No. She sat up front or used mine." Yost's face was pale, and he sent worried glances at Eva. "I'm really sorry, Eva."

"Yeah. Me, too." Despite the slight edge to her tone indicating she was still angry, at least she hadn't quit.

Erratic behavior, bookkeeping errors and not showing up for work all pointed to one thing in particular.

Drugs. He was fairly certain Eva's sister had got herself hooked on drugs. Worse, she'd likely stolen some from her supplier.

The impact of her poor choices had not only caused Malina to be killed but had reached Eva, as well.

He needed to figure out who Malina had taken the package from, and soon.

Before anyone else ended up hurt or, worse, dead.

Reeling from hearing the truth about her sister, Eva struggled to hold herself together. She didn't want to believe the things Wade claimed Malina had done. Didn't want to consider the fact that her sister might have got involved in something nefarious.

Still, it was impossible to ignore the truth staring her in the face. Wade had fired Malina. Her sister had lied to her. And now Cocoa was missing. All because of a stupid package.

Looking back, she had to admit that Malina had seemed distant a couple of months before her death. Preoccupied. Sometimes excited and other times depressed. At the time, Eva had assumed that Malina's diminishing eyesight was the reason for her behavior. Even when it came to the accident, she'd thought that Malina must not have seen the car swerving toward her until it was too late.

What if she was wrong? What if the accident had been deliberate? Eva shivered.

"Do we have time to drop off the evidence before picking up Mikey?" Finn's voice broke into her thoughts.

"I don't think so," she said, glancing at her watch. She wore one with a large face with the numbers in bold. "The traffic seems to be picking up and we're closer to the preschool than we are to your headquarters."

"Okay, we'll pick up Mikey first." Finn took the next right, toward the preschool. "How are you doing? I'm sure this hasn't been easy for you."

She let out a heavy sigh. "I'll be fine, although

it's hard to believe Malina would have got mixed up with drugs."

"It can happen to anyone," Finn said. "Try not to hold it against her."

Eva hadn't told Finn about her retinitis pigmentosa or about the fact that Malina had suffered the same progressive disorder. Was her impending blindness the reason her sister had turned to drugs? It didn't jibe with what she knew about Malina. How her sister had worried about her ability to take care of Mikey and whether or not Pete would continue being supportive.

Pete. Surely, if Malina was using drugs her husband would have known? Granted, the same thing could be said about Eva, but Malina and Pete were living in the same household day in and day out. It would have been much harder to hide something like drug abuse from a spouse.

At least Mikey's reference to a bad man-made sense now. She'd tried to pooh-pooh Finn's concern, but clearly the little boy had been exposed to something.

Why, Malina? Why would you risk your husband, your son, your life for something like drugs? Why?

Her desperate questions remained unanswered.

"Hi, Officer Finn!" At least Mikey seemed to be oblivious to her somber mood. "Hi, Abe!"

Abernathy licked Mikey's face, making him laugh. Upon returning to the car, Eva quickly buckled Mikey into his car seat and then slid in beside him.

Finn headed back toward the K-9 headquarters. Eva knew he was anxious to find fingerprints from the paper or the rock itself. She wanted the same thing, hating to think about what the raspy guy or the stinky guy might be doing to Cocoa.

Finn left them in the SUV with the engine running. He returned less than five minutes later. "They'll call me as soon as they get anything off the rock."

She nodded, exhaustion weighing heavy on her shoulders. Not just from the lack of sleep the night before, but from the most recent developments.

What else hadn't she known about her sister?

"Officer Finn, I'm hungry." Mikey's voice broke into her thoughts.

"We'll order dinner once we're home," Finn promised. He glanced at Eva as if half expecting an argument.

"If you're tired of ordering out, I can make grilled ham-and-cheese sandwiches," she offered.

"I love grilled ham and cheese, but ordering something might be easier. Not only do we need to do some searching, but I'd like you to look at the video tape. There's only one brief moment where a man in black comes into view, and I need you to tell me if he might be the raspy guy or stinky guy."

"Sure." She nodded and then glanced out her window, knowing that it was highly unlikely she'd be able to see the man's features clearly enough to identify him.

Mikey's chatter filled the silence as they fought the traffic back to Pete's house. Finn ordered food while Eva kept busy providing Mikey with a snack to hold him over until dinner arrived.

Finn opened his laptop computer and showed her the screen. "Here's the video," he said, hitting the play icon.

The clip was so brief she almost missed it. A man dressed in black stepped out from behind the dumpster, stared at the building for a moment and then disappeared from view.

"I'm sorry, but I don't recognize him."

"I was afraid of that," he said wryly. "But I had to ask." He put the video in reverse and paused it when the man's face was on the screen. It was a profile view, and grainy due to the distance. "How about now?"

The guy had a unibrow thing going on, but she hadn't got a clear view of his facial features. "Maybe," she hedged. "The unibrow is similar, but I wouldn't be willing to testify in a court of law."

"Okay, I understand." Finn shut down the video. "Thanks for trying."

It was on the tip of her tongue to confess about her limited vision, to tell him everything, but she just couldn't do it. Besides, her issues didn't matter one way or the other. She wasn't dating Finn. Being together like this was temporary.

Her impending blindness wasn't.

"Do you think Malina's purse might be here somewhere?" Finn asked, changing the subject.

Grateful for something to do, she jumped to her feet. "I'll check."

Leaving Finn and Abernathy to keep an eye on Mikey, she went up to the master suite. The closet was split in half, and one side held Malina's things. She rifled through them, searching for the black purse her sister favored. Finding it near the back, she pulled it out, her heart pounding. It was bulky, and heavier than she'd expected.

Was it this simple? With trembling fingers she unzipped the main pocket and drew the edges apart to see what was inside.

No package. Her shoulders slumped in defeat. There was a thick black wallet inside, which accounted for some of the weight, along with a variety of other things, including a hairbrush and makeup kit. Opening the wallet, she found the usual credit cards and several receipts. Her eyes widened when she saw there were five crisp one-hundred-dollar bills tucked inside.

Cash and a missing package didn't bode well. She wondered if the cash alone would be enough to satisfy Cocoa's captors but doubted it. She suspected the value of the package was much, much more.

Where was the puppy? And what would the men do if she couldn't find the missing package?

SIX

Finn kept an eye on Mikey playing with Abernathy while he subtly searched the playroom. Although he didn't believe Malina would hide drugs in the place where her son spent time playing, he wasn't about to make any assumptions. If she had been using, she might not have been thinking clearly. So he'd do what was needed to check this room off the list.

Maybe he should get one of the drug-sniffing K-9s here to see if they could find the drugs. That, of course, would only work if the package was actually drugs and not cash or other stolen goods.

By the time he finished with the playroom, Eva had returned from the master suite carrying a large black handbag in one hand and a wallet in the other.

"This was all I found," she said, holding up the wallet. "Five hundred dollars in cash. If the package contained drugs, it's likely gone."

He raised a brow and came over to see the crisp hundred-dollar bills. "I don't know, to be honest, five hundred doesn't seem like enough to risk a dognapping. In the world of drug dealing, it's chump change."

"She may have spent most of it," Eva said, her eyes full of sorrow and resignation. "Maybe this five hundred was all she had left. I don't want to admit that she was involved in anything criminal, but even I can see this doesn't look good."

Finn glanced at Mikey, making sure the little boy wasn't listening. He was still playing with Abernathy, who was good-naturedly taking the hugs and tail tugging without protest.

"I was thinking of arranging for one of the drug-sniffing K-9s to come sweep the house, just in case."

Her brow furrowed. "It doesn't feel right to do that while Pete's not here. It's his house, not mine. Can't we just look ourselves?"

There was a bit of logic in what Eva proposed. Bringing in a K-9 meant he should go through official channels and have a judge sign off on a search warrant. Since Eva was living here, taking care of her nephew with Pete's permission, she could search her sister's things without going through the legal system.

"Yeah, okay. For now."

Eva's face relaxed with relief, and he found himself wondering if she didn't really want to find the package her sister had taken. As soon as the thought formed, he brushed it off. From the very beginning, Eva was an innocent bystander in this mess. She'd brought Malina's purse down to show him the cash, something she could have hidden easily. He also knew she wanted very much to find Cocoa.

And the more he thought about the cash, the more he believed Eva might be onto something about the package being gone. Where else would Malina have got that much cash? Five hundred wasn't much for a drug dealer, but it was to your average citizen. Malina hadn't been working. If she was a drug user, the money wouldn't have lasted long.

"I'll take a look through the kitchen," Eva offered, interrupting his thoughts.

"Sure." He forced himself to concentrate on the issue at hand. "I'll check the living room."

They went their separate ways. Fifteen minutes later, when the deliveryman from Gino's Italian Ristorante arrived with their lasagna, he discovered they'd both come up empty-handed.

"I'm sure it's gone," Eva said morosely. "How will we get Cocoa back if we can't find it?"

"Cocoa?" Mikey echoed.

Eva winced, and he realized she hadn't meant to say that in front of the boy. "Officer Finn and Abernathy are still looking for him," she promised. "They'll find Cocoa."

Finn helped unpack the food, then took the seat to Eva's right, placing her between him and Mikey. "I have a good idea about what we need to do," he said, holding out his hand. "We'll pray."

Eva stared at his open palm for a long moment, before placing her hand in his. With her other hand, she reached for Mikey's. "I'm willing to try."

The little boy didn't seem to understand the concept of prayer, but at least this time he was paying attention. Finn wrapped his fingers gently around hers and bowed his head. "Dear Lord, we ask that You bless this food we are about to eat. We also ask for Your strength and guidance as we continue to search for truth and justice. We ask You to guide us on the right path to find Cocoa and to bring him home safely. Amen."

"Amen," Eva said.

"Amen," Mikey mimicked. "Cocoa safe."

That made Finn smile. "Yes. God will keep us all safe. Now we can eat."

"Noodles!" Mikey gestured with his chubby hand. "I want noodles."

"I know you do," Eva agreed wryly. "They're one of your favorites."

"Nothing wrong with his appetite," Finn said, grinning at the boy. "He's holding up really well."

Eva's expression softened. "Yes, he is. He still has the occasional nightmare, but overall is adjusting well."

"Don't like nightmares," Mikey said, tomato sauce and cheese smeared along his cheek. "Good dreams, right, Mommy?"

Eva froze at the little boy's slip, but then she leaned forward to press a kiss on his forehead. "Yes, Mikey. Good dreams."

Finn watched the interplay between Eva and Mikey, thinking about how his own mother had abandoned him all those years ago. He only vaguely remembered being hugged and kissed by her, accompanied by a hint of perfume. She'd seemed to love him the way Eva obviously loved Mikey, and to this day he couldn't understand how his mother could have just walked away. Oh, sure, he'd found her eventually, happily married to a businessman with two pretty little daughters, who were eleven and twelve years younger than him. He'd watched them for a long time, his mother smiling with her second family after abandoning the first.

He'd considered confronting her, forcing her to acknowledge him and what she'd done, but in the end he'd simply walked away without letting her know he'd been there.

"You look sad, Finn," Eva said. "What's wrong?"

"Nothing." He forced a smile and took a bite of his lasagna. "Yum. Mikey is right—this is amazing."

She tipped her head to the side, studying him thoughtfully. He fidgeted in his seat, feeling as if her blue eyes could see through his outward jovial facade to the depths buried beneath. To the secrets he'd never told anyone.

To the family he'd always wanted and at the same time refused to allow himself to have.

He was a cop. It was all he'd ever wanted. To be like his father. To protect and serve.

But watching Eva, so stunningly beautiful he could barely stand it, hug and kiss Mikey made him want to reconsider his priorities. Was it possible for him to have both his career and a family? As if sensing his inner turmoil, Abernathy came over and nudged him, placing his head in Finn's lap.

He stroked his K-9 partner's silky fur and reaffirmed this was what he was meant to be. A K-9 cop focused on bringing the bad guys to justice.

Not a family man.

Eva sensed there was something bothering Finn, but he clearly wasn't interested in sharing whatever thoughts were weighing on his mind.

For some odd reason, Finn's prayer had touched her deeply, unexpectedly providing a sense of calmness in a chaotic world. The distress she'd felt at finding the cash in Malina's purse was replaced with a sense of peace after Finn's prayer.

It occurred to her that Mikey deserved a chance to learn about God and faith. She knew Pete hadn't grown up with religion, and that he and Malina hadn't attended church on a regular basis after their wedding five years ago.

Her cell phone rang, startling her. After warily picking up the device, she relaxed when she saw Pete's name on the screen. "Hello?"

"Hi, Eva. How is Mikey doing?" Her brother-in-law's voice was difficult to hear amid the background noise.

"He's great. Do you want to talk to him?"

"Sure. I'll try to find a quiet corner." The background noise muted a bit and she held the phone out toward Mikey, putting the call on speakerphone.

"Mikey, say hi to your daddy," she instructed.

"Hi, Daddy," the child said.

"Hi, Mikey. I love you, buddy. Are you being good for Auntie Eva?"

Mikey nodded his head, apparently not understanding his father couldn't see him.

"Say yes," she encouraged.

"Yes, Daddy. When are you coming home?"

"In a few days, buddy." Pete's voice thickened with emotion. "I miss you, Mikey. Be a good boy and I'll see you soon."

"Okay, bye, Daddy."

Eva took the speaker function off and put the phone to her ear. "Listen, Pete, I need to ask you a quick question about Malina."

"What about her?" Was it her imagination or was there a hint of defensiveness in his tone?

She hesitated, glancing at Finn. He gave her a nod of encouragement, so she moved away from the table, out of Mikey's earshot and continued. "Malina may have mentioned the newest puppy I'm caring for, a chocolate Lab named Cocoa. Well, he's missing. He was taken by a thug who threw a rock through the bedroom window in the house I share with my roommates. The rock had a threatening note attached, telling me if I wanted to see the dog alive I needed to find the package my sister stole from them."

"Package? What package?" Pete asked, confusion lacing his tone.

"I don't know. I have a K-9 cop, Finn Gallagher, and his yellow Lab, Abernathy, helping to find Cocoa, but we need to know what Malina was involved in before she died."

Pete was silent for a long moment. "I don't know anything about a package. Malina and I…were going through a rough patch for a few months before she was struck by that car."

Hearing him admit that much sent a chill down her spine. "What were you two fighting about?"

"Just the usual." Pete's voice was evasive. "Nothing major, but we had a big argument about a week before the accident. Now I wish I hadn't yelled at her like that. It's all I can think of now that she's gone."

Eva sensed Pete didn't know about the five hundred dollars she'd found in Malina's wallet.

"I'm sorry to pry into your personal life, Pete. The reference to the stolen package is confusing to me. You're sure you don't know anything about a package?"

"I'm sure. I never saw Malina with a package." Pete's tone was firm. "Is Mikey really doing okay? I'm worried about how he's adjusting."

She glanced over her shoulder at the little boy liberally smeared with pasta sauce. "He's holding up very well. Try not to worry about us."

"This package business is worrisome," Pete admitted. "Maybe I should just leave the conference and come home."

"I don't think that's necessary and I wouldn't want you to get in trouble with your boss. As the paramedic training coordinator, you have to learn what's new. I have the police looking for Cocoa, and Mikey is doing great. I promise to call if that changes."

"Yeah, okay. But please be careful, Eva. Mikey needs you now more than ever. You're the only mother figure he has at the moment."

Tears pricked her eyes at the concern in Pete's tone. "I'll be very careful. See you in a few days, okay?"

"Yeah. Bye."

Pete disconnected from the line and she stared at the blank screen of her phone for a long moment, her emotions churning. She couldn't imagine what her brother-in-law was going through, losing his wife and becoming a single parent overnight. She was glad she could be there for him and for Mikey.

What was the usual stuff married couples fought about? Money? Spending time together? Or had Pete suspected drugs? She knew from her nursing roommates how the opioid crisis was infiltrating every corner of the city. How people got addicted to painkillers and, when they couldn't get the pills any longer, turned to either heroin or cocaine because they were cheaper and easier to get.

Malina had got her appendix out about five months ago. Was it possible her sister had somehow become addicted to painkillers? An addiction that had sent her searching for something cheaper and more readily available?

"Eva? Everything okay?"

"Huh?" She lifted her head and focused her gaze on Finn. "Yes, fine. Pete doesn't know anything about a package. And while he admitted to fighting with her over the usual stuff, whatever that means, he didn't say a word about Malina using drugs."

"Are you sure he'd tell you something like that?" Finn's question cut through her like a knife.

"Yes, I'm sure." She brushed past Finn to return to the kitchen although her appetite had vanished.

After Mikey was finished eating, she looked

at the mess he'd made and sighed. "Bath time," she said with a smile.

"I'll clean up in here," Finn offered. They hadn't said much during the remainder of the meal.

"Thanks." She picked up her nephew and carried him upstairs to the bathroom, wondering if Finn planned on re-searching the areas of the house she'd done. As a cop, she knew he had to be suspicious of everything, but it still hurt that he'd think the worst of her—and of Pete.

Mikey enjoyed splashing in the bathtub, and Eva had to smile at how he played with the bubbles. When the water went cool, she lifted him out, dried him off and dressed him in his jammies.

When she returned downstairs, she found Finn and Abernathy waiting in the now-spotless kitchen. "I didn't want to leave without telling you."

"Thanks for cleaning up."

"I'll come by to pick you and Mikey up again in the morning," he offered. "Unless I'm called away for something."

"Okay." It seemed foolish to turn down a ride that was intended to keep her and Mikey safe. "Let me know."

"I will." Finn stared at her intently for a moment, then turned toward the door. "Come, Abernathy."

"Bye, Abe," Mikey called out.

"Bye, Mikey," Finn said with a smile.

It was tempting to ask Finn and Abernathy to stay overnight, but she told herself that it wasn't smart to get any more emotionally involved with Finn than she already was.

Still, after he left, the silence in the house seemed suffocating.

Just like the night before, she didn't sleep well. Thankfully, Mikey slept through the night. She'd heard from Pete that he sometimes woke up with nightmares. Still, she couldn't stop thinking about the moment the rock had crashed through her window and how she'd initially thought it might be the sound of gunfire.

As a result, Eva overslept, having fallen into a deep sleep at some time after three in the morning. She quickly showered and changed, and then fed Mikey cereal for breakfast. Finn arrived and drove them to Mikey's preschool, and then he dropped her off at the training center.

"I'll call to let you know if I'm able to drive you home, okay?" Finn's expression reflected his regret. "Unfortunately, there are a few things going on that I have to take care of."

"That's fine," she assured him. "I know you have a job to do."

Though he looked like he wanted to argue, he simply nodded. She headed inside and spent the day working with George, the black Lab puppy who was a week younger than Cocoa. When Finn called to let her know he couldn't pick her up, she understood.

Taking the subway for the first time since the incident at the training center was unnerving. The dark clouds hanging overhead, an indication of an impending rainstorm, only added to her depressed mood. She found herself acutely aware of the people around her. She didn't smell the dusty, the raspy guy or the stinky, twangy guy, but for all she knew they'd sent someone else to watch over her.

Being surrounded by strangers was suffocating, and she couldn't help wondering how she'd manage to ride the train once she'd lost her eyesight. Her determination to remain independent wavered in the face of what that really meant.

Moving around Queens, among the people and traffic, seemed a daunting task. Even with a guide dog. That was what she trained them to do, but experiencing it firsthand wouldn't be easy.

Time ticked by slowly before she arrived at the subway stop near Mikey's preschool. She exited the station and waited for the stoplight to turn green. After crossing the street, she headed down the sidewalk toward the preschool.

She smelled a hint of dust seconds before a man wearing black stepped out from between two buildings and grabbed her arm roughly, yanking her into the alley and up against the wall. He was behind her, so she couldn't see his face.

"Did you find the package yet?" he whispered harshly in her ear.

"No, but I'm looking for it," she admitted, realizing this was the raspy-voiced guy, the one who had tried to drag her into the black sedan. "I promise to keep searching."

"You better look harder or you'll never see that puppy again. And you never know who'll be next."

"I'm trying," she insisted. Was the threat against her? Or Mikey?

The raspy guy yanked her from the wall and shoved her sideways. The momentum sent her falling hard against the concrete.

Her hands and knees stung from the force of the blow, but she ignored the pain, jumped up quickly and headed out to see which way he went.

The raspy guy was long gone. She struggled to breathe against a wave of panic. Fearing the stinky guy might be nearby, she turned and ran to the safety of Mikey's preschool before using her phone to call Finn.

"Gallagher."

She tried to control her racing heart. "It's Eva. The raspy guy just threatened me, or maybe Mikey. I'm at the preschool now, but I need you to come and get us. *Hurry!*"

"I'll be right there," he promised.

"Thank you." She disconnected from the call and leaned heavily against the wall near the doorway. Knowing Finn was on the way wasn't as comforting as it should be.

You never know who'll be next.

The subtle threat against her or, worse, a three-year-old boy was nearly her undoing. If anyone was the true innocent in all this, it was Mikey. These men wouldn't stop until they got what they wanted.

No matter the cost.

SEVEN

"I have to go." Finn glanced at a fellow K-9 cop, a rookie named Faith Johnson and her partner, Ricci, a German shepherd named after fallen Officer Anthony Ricci. They'd been searching the Rego Park area because someone had reported seeing a German shepherd running loose. The K-9 team had hoped the dog might be Jordan Jameson's missing K-9 partner, Snapper. So far, they'd come up empty-handed. "You'll be okay?"

"Yeah, Ricci and I will be fine." Faith waved him off. "We'll do one more sweep, then head back to headquarters before the storm." She sighed. "I was really hoping to find Snapper."

Finn nodded, but his mind wasn't on the mystery surrounding the missing K-9. He needed to get over to Mikey's preschool as soon as possible. Knowing that the raspy guy had accosted Eva and threatened her and Mikey so close to the preschool made his blood boil.

Bad enough that they'd dognapped Cocoa, but

to threaten an innocent woman and a three-year-old child? The two men must be desperate to get their package back, and he knew only too well that desperate men did equally desperate things.

Traffic was horrible, and it hadn't even started raining yet, but thankfully Rego Park wasn't far from Forest Hills, so he made it to the preschool quickly. When he and Abernathy walked up, Eva came out from the doorway, where he surmised she'd watched and waited for him. Her eyes were wide with fear and horror.

He instinctively pulled her into his arms, cradling her close. "Are you sure you're okay?"

She nodded her head, her voice muffled against his chest. "Bruised and sore, that's all."

He closed his eyes, thanking God for keeping Eva safe. He never should have let her head home alone. He should have told her to wait for him until he'd finished searching for Snapper. "I'm so sorry," he whispered.

"It's not your fault." She lifted her head to gaze up at him, her eyes bright with unshed tears. "I'm worried about Mikey. We have to find that stupid package, Finn. We have to!"

"Shh, it's okay. We'll keep looking, I promise." He pressed a gentle kiss to her temple. "Mikey is inside?"

She sniffled, swiped at her eyes and nodded. "They were working on a finger-painting project for Father's Day. Mikey wanted to finish it for his dad and told me it was to be a surprise. I assured him I'd wait for you and Abernathy. I also called Pete, but he didn't answer so I left a message. I didn't go into detail, because I didn't want to panic him, but I told him to call me back as soon as possible."

Finn nodded and glanced around the sidewalk. "Show me where this went down."

Eva looked a little nervous, so he took her hand in his, noting the rough abrasions on her palm. She led him two blocks away from the preschool and gestured to the narrow alleyway between two buildings. "Here. He grabbed me as I was walking past and shoved me up against the brick building."

Thinking about how frightened she must have been had him clenching his jaw to keep his temper in check. As if the bruise darkening her cheek wasn't bad enough, these guys just kept coming after her. He swept his gaze around the area, but there was nothing resembling a clue as to who raspy guy might be. Finn wished he had the tire iron that was used at the guide dog training center with raspy guy's scent on it, but he'd left it at the crime lab.

With a resigned sigh, he turned back toward Eva. "Okay, we have to assume he's been following you and knows the location of Mikey's preschool. I'll take you and Mikey home, and you'll need to stay there. It's too risky to continue bringing him here and going to work. I'll make sure the cops drive past the place on a regular basis."

She never hesitated. "I know. I'd never forgive myself if something happened to Mikey. His safety has to be my primary concern."

He wouldn't be able to forgive himself either if anything happened to Mikey or Eva. He took her hand again. "I'll keep you both safe. Let's get Mikey."

The little boy greeted them enthusiastically, proudly displaying his finger painting for them to see. Amid the blue-and-green swirls, the child had drawn a family portrait. There were stick figures of a man and a woman with long hair each holding the hand of a little boy who looked just like Mikey. "Auntie Eva, will you help me hide it from my dad? I want it to be a surprise."

"Of course," Eva assured him as they walked to the vehicle. Finn could tell she was getting choked up all over again. "How about if we frame it and wrap it up for him? I'm sure he'd love to have your painting hanging on the wall."

"I'd like that." Mikey grinned as she placed him in the car seat. "Can we do that today?"

"Um, maybe not today, but soon." Eva glanced at Finn and he nodded in agreement.

"I have a day off coming up, I'll be happy to take you and your aunt to get the picture framed."

"Can Abe come, too?"

"Sure."

"Goody!" Mikey clapped his hands. "I love Abe."

Finn almost told Mikey he and Abe loved him, too, but held back, reminding himself that he wasn't part of Mikey's family. A family he'd decided was not meant for him because of his career, but now couldn't stop thinking about.

He concentrated on navigating the traffic to reach Pete's home. Earlier that morning, he'd looked into Pete Stallings's background but hadn't found anything unusual. The guy appeared on paper to be just as Eva claimed, a dedicated firefighter and paramedic who loved his son. There were some money problems, but nothing too terrible. And if Malina was using drugs, the money problems made sense.

He'd pulled the autopsy results on Malina's death, too, but surprisingly, the medical examiner had not found any track marks indicating IV drug use. There was some indication that she might have been snorting cocaine, but there hadn't been any hard evidence of recent use. Damaged nasal passages could be from severe allergies as well as cocaine, especially if the user was early in the level of abuse.

All of which brought Finn back to the immediate threat. Did the two men who'd assaulted Eva know that she was staying at Pete's place? He had to assume they did. After all, they knew Malina had stolen their mysterious package. What was to prevent them from breaking into Pete's to look for the package themselves?

Unless they already had? Was it possible they'd managed to get inside the house to do their own search? And when they hadn't found what they were looking for, had gone after Cocoa and Eva? And maybe, now, Mikey?

His gut told him it was a distinct possibility.

Once he and Abernathy had Eva and Mikey safe inside the house, he decided to go through the entire place one more time. Leaving Eva and Mikey in the kitchen, eating a snack of animal crackers and milk, he took Abernathy and started up in the master suite.

He and Abernathy made their way through the upper level without finding a thing. Downstairs, he went through the living room, the playroom, bathroom, finally ending up in the kitchen.

"I already went through all the cupboards," Eva said wearily.

"I know." He glanced over his shoulder at her. "I just feel like I need to do something."

"Me, too." Her sad smile squeezed his heart. "All finished, Mikey? You want to play?"

"Yep."

She washed Mikey's face and hands, then lifted him from his booster seat. For a moment she snuggled him close, kissing his cheek, before setting him on the floor. He gave Abernathy a pat on the head, then ran toward the playroom, laughing when the K-9 followed.

Eva dropped her chin to her chest for a moment, as if struggling to remain composed. Finn couldn't stand seeing her distress. He pulled her into his arms once again, marveling at how right it felt to hold her.

"I'm sorry," she murmured. "I don't know what's wrong with me."

"Nothing is wrong with you, Eva." His own voice was low and husky with emotion. "You have every right to be upset. There've been nothing but threats and danger at every turn."

She didn't answer. He stroked his hand over her long silky blond hair, reveling in the softness against his fingertips and her clean citrusy scent. He ached to kiss her, but had promised himself to offer comfort, nothing more.

Even if it killed him, which was a distinct possibility.

After several long moments, Eva pulled out of his arms, offering a watery smile. "Thanks, Finn. You've been incredible through all of this." She surprised him by going up on tiptoe to press a soft kiss against his cheek before stepping away. "I feel safe with you and Abernathy, here."

"I'll stay for as long as you'd like," he offered rashly, willing to do anything if she kissed him like that again. Yeah, it wasn't smart to stick around where he'd only get more emotionally attached. If he had one single functioning brain cell in his head, he'd assign someone else to protect her and the boy.

But even as the fleeting thought went through his mind, he rejected it. He didn't want anyone else here watching over them.

He trusted only himself and his K-9 partner, Abernathy, to keep them safe from harm.

Once again, he lifted his heart in prayer that God would help watch over them, too.

Leaving Finn's embrace was the hardest thing she'd ever had to do. As she went into the playroom to check on Mikey, she put her hands over her warm cheeks, willing the crazy attraction away.

How was it possible to feel so attached to the man in such a short period of time? She hadn't felt this emotionally connected to a man before, not even Rafe Del Rosa. It was easy to look back and acknowledge that they'd had some fun, shared a love of art—and that was about it. No wonder he'd broken things off when learning about her retinitis pigmentosa.

She needed to tell Finn about her condition, sooner rather than later. But after the emotional turmoil of the day, she didn't want to open up that subject. Especially since once he knew the truth, those hugs and chaste kisses would likely end.

Be honest, she told herself sternly. *The main*

reason you kissed Finn on the cheek was because you were hoping he'd kiss you in return.

Yeah, okay, so what? Kissing wasn't a crime. And it had been so long since she'd met a man she truly liked. Respected. Admired.

"Can I play outside in my sandbox?" Mikey asked.

"Not today. Looks like rain." She went over to the small television in the corner of the room. "How about if I put on some cartoons for you?"

"Okay."

Once Mikey was settled on the floor, lying next to Abernathy to watch television, she returned to the kitchen to think about dinner. Malina had been the cook; Eva was more of a carryout kind of woman. But for Mikey's sake, she should at least try to provide a homemade meal. Especially since they were going to be housebound for the foreseeable future.

She opened the fridge and peered inside, hoping for inspiration.

"Hey, what if we head over to Griffin's for dinner?" Finn offered.

She closed the fridge and turned to face him, wrinkling her nose. "I don't know—it looks like rain. Besides, I can't bear the idea of being followed by the raspy guy or stinky guy or anyone else who might be looking for that stupid package."

Finn nodded. "I hear you, but Griffin's diner

is a cop hangout, I don't think anyone would be dumb enough to try anything there. And you and Mikey won't be alone—Abernathy and I will be with you the whole time. Along with plenty of other cops."

She'd never been to Griffin's but had heard it was a cop hangout. Cooking wasn't her forte, and going someplace to eat rather than going for takeout once again held a certain appeal. Yet she didn't want to do anything that might put Mikey in harm's way, either.

"It's located just a couple of blocks from the K-9 headquarters," Finn added. "I'll park there, and we can walk over."

"Okay, let's do it," she agreed. "I can't lie, my cooking is atrocious."

Finn laughed, and despite her earlier assault, she found herself smiling in return. "I'm actually not a bad cook," he said modestly, "But it would take too long to get groceries and to start a meal from scratch. I know Mikey's safety is most important and a cop hangout near our K-9 headquarters is the only place that fits the bill."

"All right. I'll get Mikey's raincoat."

Ten minutes later, they were tucked in Finn's K-9 SUV and heading back toward the K-9 headquarters. Eva remembered seeing Griffin's, when she'd been at the K-9 Command Center.

A light rain was falling, the air thick with humidity. Welcome to summer in Queens. After parking at headquarters, Finn and Abernathy escorted them down the few blocks until they reached the diner, an old redbrick building that had aged to a deep rusty brown over the years.

The interior of the café was a typical diner decor, royal blue vinyl seats in the booths, and wooden tables and chairs in the open area. Beyond that, it wasn't typical at all. There were two sides to the place. One side appeared to be a dog friendly patio, shielded from the weather by an aluminum rooftop and walls that were little more than screens that were open in the nice weather. It was homey, and she could understand why the K-9 cops liked it here. A pretty woman greeted them at the hostess stand, a large diamond ring flashing on the fourth finger of her left hand. Eva told herself that it was petty to be jealous of this woman's happiness.

"Hey, Violet, how are you?" Finn turned and pulled Eva close. "I'd like you to meet Eva Kendall and Mikey Stallings. Eva, this is Violet Griffin. She's Lou Griffin's daughter."

"Nice to meet you." Eva shook Violet's hand. "Let me guess, your father owns the restaurant?"

"Yes, he does." Violet's smile didn't reach her eyes and she glanced at Finn, who frowned as if he'd noticed too. "Dad is here, Finn, if you'd like to talk to him. You know how he likes to keep up on the cop gossip. Follow me. We're busy, but there's a table available in the doghouse."

"The doghouse?" It took a moment for the pun to register in Eva's brain. The sign above the French doors helped. It read The Dog House—Reserved for New York City's Finest.

"Sounds good. Thanks, Violet." Finn held out Eva's chair for her and then glanced around. "We'll need a booster seat, too."

"Got it." Violet returned a few minutes later with a booster seat, a paper place mat and three crayons. "For Mikey, to keep him busy."

"Thanks." Eva was grateful for her thoughtfulness.

"Finn, where have you been?" An older man with grizzled ruddy features and a shock of white hair came over to shake Finn's hand. "Haven't seen you all week."

"Been busy," Finn agreed. "This is Eva Kendall and her nephew, Mikey Stallings." After the quick round of introductions, Finn added, "Hey, Lou, are the rumors true?"

"Rumors?" The older man's attempt to sound surprised was abysmal.

"Yeah. Zach Jameson mentioned something about how you were offered a lot of money by a real estate developer for this place. Did you really turn it down?"

"Zach should learn to keep his mouth shut," Lou muttered, avoiding the question. The older man glanced back over his shoulder at his daughter. "Although I have to admit, he makes my Violet very happy. The Jamesons are a fine family, such a shame about Chief Jordan. Honestly, I couldn't ask for a better soon-to-be son-in-law."

"So you're not selling," Finn pressed.

"Not yet," Lou admitted. He waved a hand. "Go on now, enjoy your meal."

A waitress came by to take their order. Eva ordered a burger and Finn ordered the same. Mikey wanted chicken strips and a glass of chocolate milk.

"It's nice they allow dogs here in the patio area," she said once their server left to place their order.

"Yeah, well, being so close to our headquarters helped. Lou quickly figured out that half his business came from K-9 cops, so he added this outdoor patio for customers with dogs. And he constructed it in a way that it can be sheltered from the elements." Finn glanced down at Abernathy lying on the floor between his seat and Mikey's. "The dogs are all very well trained, so it hasn't been a problem."

"It's a nice place," she agreed.

"Yeah, Lou treats us all like we're his kids, checking up on us and making sure we're doing okay." He leaned forward and lowered his voice. "That's why everyone is upset to hear some rich real estate mogul wants to buy the building. We're hoping Lou doesn't cave to the temptation to sell."

She nodded, understanding his point. Mikey

continued coloring his picture while they waited for their food. Despite how busy the place was, their meals arrived quickly. She cut up Mikey's chicken so it would cool off.

"Let's say grace," Finn said, picking up her hand and Mikey's. "Dear Lord, bless this food we are about to eat. And provide guidance to Lou as he decides his future. Amen."

"Amen," she echoed, feeling self-conscious about praying in public. Then she realized she needn't have worried. No one seemed to pay them any attention, and, to her surprise, she noticed another couple at a table several rows back also praying before their meal.

"Yummy," Mikey said, taking a bite of his crispy chicken.

"My burger is good, too," she confided.

A few minutes into their meal the sound of raised voices from the other side of the restaurant caught Finn's attention. With a frown, he rose to his feet. "Stay here, we'll be right back."

He and Abernathy made their way over to where two men were arguing loudly. Eva craned her neck, trying to see what was going on. She stood to get a better view, gasping in horror when she noticed one of the men punch the other one in the face mere inches from Finn.

"Who starts a fight in a café known to be a cop hangout?"

She was talking to herself, as everyone's attention was centered on the ruckus. She took a step forward, not liking the thought of Finn getting in the middle of a fight. But she needn't have worried. Between Finn and a man she assumed was another cop, they managed to separate the two men, each slapping cuffs on their respective perpetrator.

Relieved the crisis was over, Eva turned back to the table, looking for Mikey. His chair was empty.

"Mikey? Mikey!" She shouted to be heard over the din, raking her gaze around the restaurant. But there was no sign of the boy.

Mikey was gone!

EIGHT

"Finn!" The panic in Eva's voice caught his attention. He released the guy he'd just handcuffed, pushing him toward Ian, one of his fellow officers, to look over toward Eva. "Mikey's gone!"

"Gone?" He and Abernathy charged past the diner onlookers to reach her side. "What happened?"

"I don't know!" Eva's blue eyes were wild with fear. She gripped his arms tightly. "I turned my back on him for only a minute when I thought that man was going to punch you in the face. When I looked back, he was gone. It's my fault, Finn. This is all my fault!"

"No, it's not." Fighting a sense of panic himself, Finn surveyed the patio, then the interior of the diner, thinking it was possible the child had decided to head to the bathroom. He hurried over to check, but the restrooms were empty. There was no sign of the little boy's blond head anywhere in sight. Returning to the table, Finn's gaze landed on the child's blue raincoat draped over the seat. He grabbed it.

"Find, Abernathy," he commanded, opening the coat so that his K-9 partner could sniff the interior closest to where Mikey's skin had been. "Find Mikey."

Abernathy buried his nose in Mikey's raincoat for several long moments. Finn knew that Mikey's scent was well-known to Abernathy, considering how much time they'd spent at Pete's house, but this was part of the K-9 training process, signifying they were on the job.

Abernathy put his nose to the ground around the chair Mikey had used. He alerted there, but Finn encouraged him to keep going. The K-9 followed the invisible trail of Mikey's scent through the open patio space to the sidewalk outside the diner. Finn's stomach clenched as he realized that despite his assurances to Eva that she and Mikey would be safe here, he'd been wrong.

So very, very wrong.

"Find, Abernathy," he encouraged, following the K-9 outside. Similar to the day of Cocoa's dognapping, the dog turned and headed down the sidewalk to the next intersection. There, Abernathy sniffed along the ground, turning in a circle before sitting down. When the Lab looked up, Finn thought he perceived a concerned and pleading expression in the dog's dark eyes, as if he was waiting for the next command.

"I know. I'm worried about him, too." Finn bent over to give Abernathy a quick rub and a treat before leading him back to the doorway of Griffin's diner.

"He lost the trail?" Eva's hopeful expression collapsed, and her eyes filled with tears. "I can't believe this is happening. What if they hurt him, Finn? He's just a little boy! We need to find him!"

"I'll call the team. We'll have all officers drop whatever they're doing to search for Mikey." He used his radio to call for backup, putting out the word that a three-year-old child had been taken from Griffin's. He requested an Amber Alert, too, informing the dispatcher of what Mikey had been wearing. A red-and-white-striped shirt with navy shorts and slip-on athletic shoes.

"Eva, do you have a recent picture of him on your phone?"

She nodded and quickly texted it to him. He in turn sent it to the dispatcher to use for the Amber Alert.

Within five minutes, additional cops and their respective K-9 partners arrived. He held out Mikey's raincoat to the newcomers—Carter Jameson and his white German shepherd, Frosty, Reed Branson and his bloodhound, Jessie, and Tony Knight and his chocolate Lab, Rusty. They were the first three responders, and he was grateful that each of their K-9s were trained to follow a very specific scent.

Even those who weren't would join in the search, but he appreciated the extra expertise.

"Use Mikey's raincoat for his scent," he directed. He wasn't the highest-ranking officer there but took charge anyway. "Abernathy followed the trail outside to the intersection. The scent ended there, and I'm afraid that likely means the kidnapper had a ride waiting for him. We need to divide up the city, searching quadrant by quadrant."

"Done," Carter Jameson agreed, concern darkening his eyes. "You're taking charge of this operation, so let us know where you want everyone to go."

A feeling of helplessness washed over him. The two men who'd taken Cocoa and now Mikey could be anywhere in the massive city of New York. He hoped and prayed that concentrating on the Queens borough was the right thing to do. It made sense to him that these guys must be staying somewhere close by. Especially considering how frequently they'd been striking out at Eva and those around her.

Carter pulled out a map of Queens and spread it on the table. Finn bent over it, concentrating on the best strategy. "I'd like to take Forest Hills, since that's where a lot of the incidents took place." He glanced up at the three officers surrounding him. "Carter, I'd like you to take

Rego Park. Reed, maybe you and Jessie could take Corona."

"You want me and Rusty to take Elmhurst?" Tony Knight asked. "Those are the three closest areas to where we are now. Assuming that the bad guys are smart enough to stay away from Jackson Heights, since that's where our headquarters is located."

"Sure, although I'd like officers to stay around here, too. Griffin's is the location of the crime, so we can't ignore it." There was so much ground to cover, and the bad guys had a vehicle to go wherever they wanted. Yet by his estimation and, apparently, the others as well, these were the most logical places to start. When more officers arrived, he doled out more assignments until they had pretty much an entire circle around Pete's place and Griffin's covered. Between searching and putting out the Amber Alert, he thought they had a good chance of getting Mikey back soon.

The alternative was unthinkable.

"Eva, stay here at Griffin's for a while, I'll check in with you if I find anything," he said as he prepared to leave.

"No. I'm coming with you." The stubborn thrust of her chin and steely determination in her eyes made him groan. There wasn't time to argue. He wanted to hit the streets now, before too much time had passed.

Each minute would feel like a lifetime to a three-year-old child.

"Fine," he capitulated, unwilling to waste another second. "Let's go."

Eva nodded. She accompanied him outside as they hurried back to his SUV. The drive to Forest Hills took longer than he wanted, but his gut told him that these two men would be staying someplace close. They'd accosted Eva near the preschool and at the training center, both located in Forest Hills. This was the place he knew instinctively they'd be found.

"This is all my fault," Eva said in a low, tortured tone. "I never should have taken my eyes off Mikey, not for a second."

"It's my fault for suggesting we go to Griffin's in the first place," he countered in a grim tone. "I thought we'd be safe surrounded by so many cops. Stupid to assume any such thing."

Eva shook her head. "I'm the one responsible for watching over Mikey in Pete's absence." She pulled out her cell phone. "I need to call him again, before he hears about it on the news."

Knowing the Amber Alert would go out on the local news and possibly be picked up by the national networks, he nodded. This time she reached Pete, who'd tried to call her earlier, but she must have missed his call while in the noisy diner. Listening to her side of the conversation, it was easy to hear the alarm in Pete's voice after Eva explained what had happened.

"I can't believe they kidnapped my son!"

"I'm so sorry, Pete. I failed you and Mikey." Eva's voice grew thick with tears.

"Ask for permission for a drug-sniffing K-9 to search his house," he whispered. Finding the missing package would be the best way to negotiate with Mikey's kidnappers.

She did, and Pete must have calmed down some, because Eva nodded to him. "We'll let you know if we find anything," she promised.

Finn missed the next part of the conversation.

"If you can get a flight home, that would be great," Eva finally said. "Just let me know when to expect you."

Finn wasn't surprised that Pete's plan was to fly home immediately. That was exactly what he would do if it was his son who had been taken. The way Eva sat looking so forlorn made him long to offer comfort. He tightened his grip on the steering wheel, willing the traffic to part like the Red Sea, allowing him through.

"Pete's never going to trust me with Mikey again."

"Eva, please stop berating yourself. The real fault lies with the men who would stoop so low as to use a child as hostage to get a package back."

Eva wiped the tears from her face. He pulled into Pete's driveway and got out from behind the wheel. After freeing Abernathy from the back, he approached Eva. Fresh tears streaked her cheeks, ripping at his heart.

"You don't understand," she said as he approached. "Remember how you asked me if I'd noticed anyone following me?"

He frowned, trying to understand where she was going with this. "Yes, but you can't beat yourself up for not noticing someone tailing you. You're not a trained police officer and, even then, clearly we were followed tonight without my knowledge. No one is invincible. And these guys could have two vehicles for all we know. Switching them out would make it even harder to find a tail."

She shook her head, looking impatient. "No, it's not that. I wasn't entirely truthful with you." She took a deep breath, as if bracing herself, before she met his gaze head-on. "I didn't tell you about the problem with my vision. About how my peripheral vision is limited. Not only that, but it's hard for me to see clearly in dim lighting. Facial features are often blurry."

He was surprised by her admission. "Is that something new you've been dealing with? Maybe you need to see an eye specialist."

"I have seen a specialist, and no, it's not anything new. I have a degenerative vision disorder called retinitis pigmentosa. It's a progressive blindness disorder that is hereditary in nature. I'll likely be deemed legally blind in three years."

Finn was shocked at the news, although it helped drop a piece of the puzzle into place. He understood now why she hadn't been able to give a detailed description to the sketch artist and why she was so in tune to the way the two men sounded and smelled rather than how they looked. "I don't understand. Why didn't you say anything before now?"

"I had my reasons, and really, none of that matters right now. I wanted you to know the truth." She glanced down at Abernathy standing patiently at his side. "Let's keep searching for Mikey."

Finn wasn't keen on the idea of dropping the subject as if it were a rotten tomato, but she was right about time being of the essence in finding the boy. Yet, as he put Abernathy to work, his thoughts whirled. Was her limited eyesight the real reason she'd pulled out of his arms earlier in the day? He didn't like thinking she was ashamed of her diagnosis.

He made a mental promise to approach the issue of her eyesight later, once they'd found Mikey safe and sound.

Eva should have felt better after telling Finn the truth, but she didn't. Plagued by guilt, she couldn't help thinking that if her eyesight had been better—or if she'd told Finn the truth before now—Mikey wouldn't have been kidnapped right under her nose.

They walked up one street and down the other, a painstaking process wherein Finn worked hard to encourage Abernathy to pick up Mikey's scent. They stopped at each apartment building, each intersection, anywhere that one of the two men who'd kidnapped the boy might be holding him hostage.

She replayed the conversation with Pete in her mind, wondering if he'd got a flight home yet. As Finn and Abernathy took another detour up to a rather run-down apartment building, she used her phone to call him.

"Did you find him?" Pete asked, his tone betraying his hope.

"Not yet," she said, feeling even more miserable. "We're doing our best, and everyone is helping in the search."

"Eva, I can't lose Mikey—I just can't." Pete's voice was full of harsh desperation. "I never should have come to this stupid conference. I don't care if I'm the training coordinator. I should have told my boss to forget about it."

"I'm sorry, Pete. I feel terrible. Did you get a flight home?"

"Not yet. There's a huge thunderstorm moving in, so there is a delay on all outgoing and incoming flights." He sounded upset, not that she blamed him. "I'm trying to find another option, see if I can rent a car to get to another city that is outside the range of the storm."

"Pete, don't do something rash," she cautioned. "The storm might blow past before you reach your next destination. Stay put for now. I'll update you on a regular basis, okay?"

There was a long silence from the other end of the line. When Finn and Abernathy turned away from the apartment building, her hopes plummeted. But she did her best to sound upbeat for Pete's sake.

"Pete? Really, we're going to find him. We have cops and search-and-rescue K-9s combing the entire Queens borough."

"This is all because of some stupid package Malina took from them?" Pete finally asked.

"Yes. I'm afraid so." She fell into step beside Finn and Abernathy. "I've searched the entire house twice but haven't found anything. Are you sure you don't know of any other hiding place Malina might use?"

"I've been racking my brain about it since you called. I don't know of anywhere she would use other than her work or our place. You have my permission to search every nook and cranny."

She wasn't sure if Pete knew Malina had been fired from the guide dog training center but decided this wasn't the time to tell him. There was something else nagging at her. "Did Malina have a gym membership?"

"She used to," Pete acknowledged. "But we stopped paying for it a few months before she died."

"Yeah, okay." She vaguely remembered Malina talking about some new gym she was going to that was located near her home. The Fitness Club. "Stay in Atlanta until it's safe to fly," she repeated. "And I'll call you as soon as I know anything."

"Thanks, Eva."

She closed her eyes momentarily, thinking that she was the last person Pete should be thanking. "We're in this together," she finally said. "And we won't rest until we find him."

"I know." Pete didn't say anything more as he disconnected from the call.

"What was that about a gym?" Finn asked.

"Malina used to go to a place called The Fitness Club to work out, but Pete says that they let their membership lapse a few months ago. I keep thinking of the stinky guy and how he reminded me of how a gym smelled." As they started down another block, Eva noticed the sun was slowly beginning to set. In another hour or two the city would be shrouded in darkness.

Her heart squeezed painfully. Surely the two men wouldn't hurt the boy, but would they understand he was afraid of the dark? Would they care enough to put a night-light on for him? Would they give him a bath and a snack before bed?

Of course they wouldn't, and the overwhelming feeling of despair almost sent her to her knees. She stumbled, instinctively reaching out for Finn.

"Eva? What's wrong?"

"I just…can't stand it. The thought of Mikey being scared and alone, it's killing me."

Finn put his arm around her shoulders, giving her a reassuring squeeze. "Let's pray for Mikey," he suggested. "Let's pray that God will watch over him, keeping him safe. That he'll be strong and brave, secure in the knowledge that we're coming for him."

"Okay," she whispered.

"Dear Lord, we ask that You please keep Mikey safe in Your loving arms. Give him the strength he needs to hang on until we can get there. Guide us on Your chosen path and provide the light we need to find him. Amen."

"Amen," she echoed. "Thank you, Finn."

"Let's keep going," he encouraged. "There's another place up ahead that has potential as a hiding spot."

She nodded and kept pace with Finn and Abernathy. As she walked, she repeated Finn's heartfelt prayer over and over in her mind.

It was strange to open her heart and her mind to God. Yet, despite her fears, she felt a slight measure of peace at knowing that Mikey wouldn't be all alone with those evil men.

God would be there with him.

The next building was a dead end, as was the next one. Abernathy worked tirelessly, and she appreciated having the K-9's keen scent offering them assistance.

She'd kept the Amber Alert on her phone, looking down at Mikey's smiling face periodically as a way to reassure herself that everything possible was being done to find him.

Fighting fatigue, she kept pace as they started down another street. Finn had identified that houses with for-sale signs were sometimes used as short-term rentals, so they went to each of those, as well.

Her phone rang again and, assuming it was Pete, she answered it quickly. "Did you get a flight?"

There was a moment's hesitation before a mechanically distorted voice said, "If you want to see the kid again, find the package."

"You have Mikey?" Her gaze clashed with Finn's, and he rotated his index finger in a way she knew meant *do everything possible to keep the caller on the line.* "How do I know he's alive? I'm not turning over anything to you without some proof that you haven't harmed the child."

"He's fine, or he will be if you bring the package," the mechanical voice repeated. "If you don't…" The caller let his voice trail off.

Eva gripped her phone harder, aware of Finn talking to headquarters, asking for a trace on her phone. There was some kind of noise in the background, but she continued to press her point. "Please, he's only three years old. Just let me talk to him for a moment. He won't be afraid if he knows I'm coming to find him."

"Find the package."

The call ended abruptly, and it took all her willpower not to throw her phone against the closest brick wall.

If she knew where the package was, she'd gladly trade it for Mikey's life. But she didn't.

And was very afraid these men wouldn't blink at hurting a little boy to make their point.

NINE

"We didn't get the trace."

Finn let out a harsh breath and drew his hand down his face at their technical specialist Danielle Abbott's response. "Thanks for trying."

"We'll keep her phone queued up so we can trace the next call."

"Thanks." He'd known tracing the call that had come in on Eva's phone was a long shot, especially since it had taken precious seconds to get the phone pinged, but he'd hoped for something—anything—they could use to find Mikey.

He hated to admit that he and Abernathy were coming up empty-handed.

"They want the package," Eva's voice was dull with resignation. "I don't understand why they haven't figured out that I would have already turned it over if I'd had it."

Finn didn't know what to say to that. If the package was drugs or money, they'd have to get permission to use it as a way to draw out the kidnappers. No way would they be allowed to simply hand it over to secure Mikey's freedom. There would be a whole task force involved, something he sensed Eva wouldn't appreciate. Since it was a moot point, he decided not to go down that path.

"What exactly did he say?"

"If I want to see Mikey again, I'll find the package." She looked as if she might cry. "He refused to let me talk to Mikey, and at the end of the call repeated the demand to find the package. I tried to see if I could hear Mikey in the background, but I can't be sure."

Adrenaline spiked as he moved a step closer. "Think, Eva. You have astute hearing. Go over the call again in your mind. Can you remember if you heard any background noises during the conversation? Anything that would give us a clue as to where Mikey is being held?"

She shook her head automatically, then frowned. "Wait, maybe."

"What was it?" He practically held his breath as he waited for her to respond.

Eva was quiet for several long moments, then she started to hum a few bars of a tune.

"It sounds familiar," he said. "Do you recognize what it's from?"

"It's a cartoon that Mikey's watched before." The hint of tears vanished from her eyes. She reached out to grasp his arm. "They wouldn't put cartoons on the television if Mikey was hurt, would they? He must be okay."

He nodded thoughtfully. "I agree. Having Mikey watch cartoons is a good way for them to keep him quiet and less likely to cause trouble."

"I'll call Pete to let him know," she said, glancing down at her phone.

"Hold off for a moment," he advised. "If you call Pete, he's going to think we found Mikey. Let's not raise his hopes up over nothing."

Her shoulders slumped, and she nodded. "You're right. It's just that even knowing this much helps."

Was he making a mistake by holding her back from contacting Pete? He wasn't sure. The cynical cop inside him couldn't help wondering if Pete had arranged for these guys to kidnap Mikey and to hold him for ransom in order to get the package back. Pete being out of town at a conference provided a rock-solid alibi.

He just kept coming back to the fact that it was difficult to believe that Pete hadn't known what Malina was doing. That she was using drugs and possibly selling them, too.

The ringing of his phone interrupted his dark thoughts, and he lifted the device to his ear, recognizing the number as coming in from the K-9 headquarters. "Gallagher."

"We got a tip about the missing kid," the dispatcher told him.

His pulse spiked and he locked gazes with Eva. "What kind of tip?"

"Some woman saw the Amber Alert. She claims she was driving by Griffin's when she saw a man dressed in black running from the patio with a child matching Mikey's description. She saw him run down the block and then jump into a midsize black sedan."

"Did she get a license plate?" He held his breath, hoping and praying that she had.

"A partial. First three letters are Bravo, Delta, Tango. She wasn't sure, but she thought the first number was five, but it also could be an eight. We checked Griffin's video and saw the car but couldn't get the plate number. We're running a trace on the partial plate now, looking for matches with a black four-door sedan."

He remembered how, a few days ago, one of the men had tried to get Eva into a vehicle. That one, too, had been a four-door sedan. Not a coincidence and the first tangible lead they'd got since Mikey's disappearance.

"That's great, thanks. Let me know when you get a list of potential matches."

"Will do." The dispatcher disconnected from the call.

"We have a license plate number?" Eva's wide eyes were full of hope. "That's good news, right? We'll be able to use that information to find Mikey?"

"It's good news, but it's not a complete license plate number. We'll be able to narrow it down to a manageable list of possibilities." He glanced up, noticing the sun was beginning to set, dipping low on the horizon. There was less than an hour of daylight left. "Let's get back to the house. They'll call when they have some information for us."

"I don't like giving up the search," Eva said in a low tone. "We need to keep looking."

He understood where she was coming from. Hadn't he felt the same way? But waiting for the partial plate information was far better than wandering aimlessly around Forest Hills. "I need to check in with the rest of the team anyway. See if anyone came up with something." When she opened her mouth to argue, he gestured toward Abernathy. "My K-9 partner needs food and water. Resting for a while until we have something more concrete to go on is the best thing for him, and for us."

Eva bent down to give Abernathy's golden-yellow fur a rub. "All right. Let's go."

The walk back to Pete's place wasn't very long because Finn had taken a circular route, with the house remaining in the center.

After providing food and water for Abernathy, he and Eva sat at the kitchen table. He noticed her gaze traveling over the kitchen, and he wondered if she was trying to find something they'd missed during the first two searches.

"Since Pete gave us permission to search, I'll ask Zach Jameson to bring Eddie, his drug-sniffing beagle, to come out." Scrolling through his contact list, he found Zach's number. "That way we'll know for sure the package isn't here. Getting our hands on that package can only help get Mikey back."

"Unless the package is money and not drugs," Eva pointed out wearily. "You're assuming they're drugs."

"One problem at a time," he said. Zach picked up on the other end of the line. "Hey, do you have time to bring Eddie out here to Forest Hills to sweep the Stallings' house for drugs? We have reason to believe that Mikey has been kidnapped in an effort to get a package of drugs back."

"Not a problem, we can be there in thirty," Zach agreed.

"Thanks." Finn gave Zach the address, then set his phone down. "Zach and Eddie are on their way."

Eva nodded, her expression troubled. Whether the package contained drugs or money didn't matter much. The money could have easily been related to buying or selling drugs. In fact, considering the money troubles he'd found in Pete Stalling's bank account, he was leaning toward a stash of cash. It made the most sense. Especially since he didn't believe Malina would have risked her son finding drugs.

Zach and Eddie made good time, arriving twenty minutes later. The K-9 partners started in the kitchen and searched the entire house, room by room. Finn followed from a distance, watching the team work. Eddie, the beagle, alerted in the master bathroom.

"We've looked here, but let's do it again," Finn said.

There were no packages but, upon further inspection, Zach found a tiny bit of white powder in the corner of the cabinet beneath the sink. "I think this must be what Eddie picked up." Zack glanced up at Finn. "We can take a sample and have it tested, but I believe it's cocaine."

"I agree." Finn watched as Zack managed to get a tiny bit of the white powder into an evidence bag, and Finn hoped it was enough to run a decent test. That Eddie had picked up on the scent was impressive. "Let's finish the upper level."

Zach nodded and instructed Eddie to find. The dog went back to work gamely, but the rest of the house was clean.

No package of drugs—or anything else.

"Thanks," Finn said. "Sorry to drag you out here for this."

"Hey, we likely found evidence of cocaine, so it was worth it." Zach's expression turned grim. "I thought we'd done a good job busting up the drug ring at the airport last month, but it's clear we only made a slight dent in the problem. I wonder if the guy who escaped is involved in this, too. We haven't found the ringleader yet, either. He's likely involved."

"We'll get him." Finn led the way down to the first floor. Eva was still in the kitchen, lightly petting Abernathy as he lay on the floor near her feet.

"Find anything?" Eva asked.

"Just a trace of white powder that needs to be tested." Finn glanced at Zach, who remained silent. "Nothing else. I think if the package is drugs, we can safely say it's not here at the house."

Eva grimaced. "I should have asked him what was in the package," she berated herself. "Next time, I'll push for an answer."

Though Finn wasn't sure there would be a next time, he nodded in agreement. "Couldn't hurt."

"I'll let you know what we find," Zach said. He and Eddie moved toward the door. "If you need anything else, holler."

"Will do." Finn walked them to the door, watching as they climbed into the K-9 SUV. It occurred to him that they should search the training center and The Fitness Club gym. He doubted either would be fruitful, but at this point he needed to cover every possibility.

No matter how remote.

Upon returning to the kitchen, his phone rang.

His heart thumped wildly as he recognized the number. "Tell me you have a plate number and address."

"We have a plate number and that led to an address—an apartment located in Forest Hills. It's registered to an R. Talmadge. Got a pen?"

Finn glanced around the kitchen, found a pen and pad of paper and began scribbling as the dispatcher gave him the address. The apartment wasn't far from Pete's house, and it galled him to know that if he'd widened his search by another block, he might have found it. "Thanks, I'm heading over there now with Abernathy. We're the closest. Send backup."

"Will do."

"I'm coming with you," Eva said as he buckled Abernathy's vest in place and clipped on the leash. The yellow Lab stretched and then sat at his side, waiting for his command.

"Not happening. It's too dangerous." He was bound and determined not to drag Eva along. Especially since darkness had fallen and he knew her vision was compromised.

"Mikey needs me. He doesn't have a mother or a father here. *He needs me.*"

What was it about her that he couldn't deny her anything? Finn swallowed an exasperated sigh. "Fine, but you better do exactly as I say. No argument. I can't allow you to be anywhere close to danger, understand?" They hurried outside to get into his SUV. "If a civilian gets hurt on my watch, my career is over."

"I won't get hurt," Eva insisted. She slid into the passenger seat as he put Abernathy in the back and then climbed behind the wheel.

He didn't want to acknowledge that keeping her safe was more important than his career, but it was. And he couldn't stand the thought of Mikey suffering at the hands of his captors. If having Eva along helped the boy adjust, then fine. He'd break the rules for a three-year-old any day of the week.

Navigating the streets to the address he'd programmed into his cell phone, Finn prayed silently that they'd find Mikey safe and unharmed.

Eva barely glanced at the apartment building Finn had double-parked in front of, intent on unbuckling her seat belt to follow him inside.

"You need to stay here," he said, releasing Abernathy from the back of the SUV. "My backup will be here any minute, but I'm going in."

"I might be able to recognize the sound of the cartoon through the door." She'd come this far and didn't see what the problem was in going the rest of the way. She'd prayed that God would show them the way to find Mikey and knew they were close. "Do you even have a clue as to what apartment number they're in?"

He scanned the mailboxes. "I don't see the

name Talmadge listed anywhere, and wasn't given one, but that's where Abernathy will help." He took out Mikey's raincoat for his K-9 partner. "Find Mikey."

Abernathy put his nose to the ground and alerted on Mikey's scent near the front doorway. Eva's heart was beating so fast she thought it might burst from her chest. The security lock was intact, so Finn pressed the buzzer for the building's superintendent, informing him he was with the police and asking him to open the door.

Abernathy seemed eager to work, sniffing along the hallways as they made their way around the ground floor. When the K-9 didn't alert on that level, they went to the second floor.

"How many floors does this place have?" she asked in a whisper.

"Ten."

Eva's hope began to wane as Abernathy didn't alert on the third floor, either. Ten floors could take forever to search.

On the fourth floor, Abernathy alerted at an apartment door halfway down the hall. Eva sucked in a quick breath as they cautiously approached. Sounds were coming through the thin doorway, and as she came closer, she heard the television.

Straining to listen, she slowly nodded at Finn when she realized the same cartoon show was still on. Maybe the men had recorded it to play over and over again to keep Mikey occupied.

"Go back outside," Finn whispered. Gently he tried the door handle, but of course it was locked. He pulled his weapon and then hammered on the door with his fist. "Police! Open up!"

Eva had begun to retreat down the hallway when she heard a series of loud thumps from inside the apartment.

No! They were going to get away!

Finn lifted his foot and kicked at the door near the handle. Once, twice. The wood frame splintered and gave way, the door swinging open beneath the pressure. Finn entered the apartment, weapon held ready with Abernathy at his side.

"Stop! Police!"

The thumping grew louder, drowning out the sound of the television. When Mikey started crying, Eva decided she wasn't leaving. Not now. Not when they were so close to finding Mikey. Ignoring Finn's directive, she followed him inside the apartment. Where was his backup? Shouldn't they be here by now?

Creeping farther into the room, the shouting from the man and Mikey's shrill screams grew louder. As she rounded the corner, she saw a man dressed in black holding Mikey in his arms as he tried to throw one leg over the windowsill.

"Get him, Abernathy!" Finn commanded.

The yellow Lab ran across the room and

latched onto the guy's ankle. Labs weren't trained as attack dogs, but she believed Abernathy sensed Mikey was in danger. The man howled in pain, which only made Mikey scream louder.

"I want my mommy!"

"Stop! Get him," Finn repeated.

Abernathy continued to tug on the man's leg, growling low in his throat. Eva kept her gaze trained on Mikey, trying to send reassuring vibes. The man wasn't very far away, half in and half out of the window. His gaze was locked on Abernathy, and he was so busy trying to shake the dog off that the gun in his right hand was pointed away from her and Finn.

It was now or never. Ignoring Finn's harsh cry to stay back, she rushed forward, grabbed Mikey and yanked him from the man's arms. The hand holding the gun came over to hit her on the shoulder at the same moment the sound of gunfire echoed through the room. It was so loud it caused a ringing in her ears.

She dropped to the floor, instinctively curling her body over Mikey's in an attempt to protect him.

"I'm here. You're safe, Mikey. It's okay, you're safe." She repeated the words over and over even as the room suddenly filled with cops. Finn came over to take her arm, helping her stand.

"I told you to stay outside!" His voice was

hoarse with fear and anger. "You almost got yourself killed!"

Mikey's crying increased in volume and she raked him with her gaze. "Not now. Yell at me later. Mikey is frightened enough. Did you get him?" She looked around the room, relieved to note that the guy was sitting in a chair, his hands cuffed behind his back. The odd dusty smell that clung to his clothing helped her identify him as the thug who'd grabbed her arm and tried to get her into the waiting car not far from Finn's headquarters.

Was he here alone? Or was the stinky guy here, too? If so, where was the puppy?

Cops swarmed the apartment quickly, searching for anyone else who might be inside. She heard one of them shout, "Clear!" and knew that meant no one else was there.

Eva sat down on the edge of the sofa, cradling Mikey close, stroking his back and whispering to him, "It's all over, sweetie. You were so brave. Abernathy was smart enough to help us find you."

Mikey's arms were wrapped so tightly around her neck it was difficult to breathe. Her shoulder from where the man had punched her, but she ignored it, refusing to release her hold on the little boy.

Too close. The gunshot had whizzed past her and Mikey before wedging into the wall. The replay of the night's events would haunt her for a long time. So many things could have gone wrong but hadn't. They'd caught one of the bad guys and rescued the little boy from harm.

As she held the precious child in her arms, Eva knew she had God to thank for keeping Mikey safe.

TEN

Upset at how Eva had rushed in to grab Mikey, Finn was also angry at himself for losing his cool. He shouldn't have yelled at her. Thankfully, everything had turned out okay. They'd found Mikey and had the perp handcuffed. He wished Eva hadn't put herself in danger but knew that, given the same set of circumstances, she'd likely do the same thing again.

Watching Eva holding Mikey on the edge of the sofa, rocking back and forth as she attempted to calm him down, he let the last vestiges of his anger go. The way Mikey was clinging to Eva only proved her point. The boy didn't have his mother or his father here, and he deserved to be comforted by Eva, the closest thing to a mother figure he had.

"We got nothing," Zach Jameson announced. "No sign of Cocoa or anyone else staying here."

Finn blew out a frustrated breath. Clearly the two men were smart enough to remain separated. As much as he wanted to find Cocoa, he couldn't help being glad they'd found Mikey so quickly. The Amber Alert had worked in their favor. Too bad there wasn't a dog version of an Amber Alert. They could put one out for Snapper and for Cocoa.

He approached the handcuffed perp on the floor. Just because the apartment was registered to Talmadge, didn't mean this was the same man. "What's your name?"

The guy stared straight ahead, refusing to make eye contact with any of the cops swarming the apartment.

"You're facing serious charges here," Finn pointed out. "Felony kidnapping, not to mention the attempted kidnapping of Eva that I witnessed a few days ago. I'm sure once we run your fingerprints through the system, we'll find other outstanding warrants. Enough to put you away for a very long time."

He noticed the perp flinch, but he still didn't look at him. Finn waited for a long moment, hoping the impact of what the man was facing would sink into his tiny brain.

"I want a lawyer." Although the perp still hadn't met his gaze, Finn had to admit his voice was indeed raspy, the way Eva had described. "Not talking till I get my lawyer."

While expected, the request didn't make him feel any better. He gestured for a couple of the beat cops who'd arrived on the scene to escort the perp out to their car. "Read him his rights and get him his lawyer. I'll meet you at the jail soon."

The two beat cops nodded and escorted the cuffed kidnapper out of the apartment. Zach and his K-9, Eddie, were still searching the place for drugs. "Gallagher! In here," Zach called, a hint of excitement in his tone.

Finn headed into the back bedroom. "Find something?"

"Eddie alerted here." Zach gestured to the bedroom closet. "I want you as a witness before going inside."

Finn nodded. "Let's do it."

Zach opened the closet door and Eddie alerted again. Finn leaned close and saw a sprinkle of white dust similar to what they'd found in the master bathroom at Pete's house. Finn glanced at Zach. "We can bag it as evidence, but I was hoping for something more substantial."

"Me, too." Zach bagged the evidence, then they went on to search the rest of the closet. Finding nothing, Zach let out a sigh. "Guess that's it, then."

"I'd like the lab to compare the two samples you collected today, the one from the house and this one, to see if they share the exact same chemical makeup," Finn said.

"Good idea." Zach raised a brow. "And if they do?"

Finn shrugged. "It's a connection. I'm not

sure what it means yet, but I don't believe in coincidences."

"True." Zach placed the evidence bag in his pocket. "Every bit of evidence counts. I'll let you know what the lab says."

"Thanks." Finn returned to the main living area of the apartment. Eva and Mikey were exactly where he'd left them. Abernathy was hovering near Mikey, trying to lick his face. The obvious affection between Mikey and his K-9 was endearing.

"Eva? Are you and Mikey ready to get out of here?"

She looked up at him with a wan smile. "Yes, please."

"I'll drive you both back to Pete's and have a cop stationed outside for protection, then I need to head back to headquarters to grill this guy. By then we should at least know who he is and maybe will get a lead on known associates."

"He's not the stinky guy," Eva said. "He doesn't smell right, have a Southern twang or scratches on his forearm. But I think he's the raspy guy."

She was right, and again he was impressed with how well she used her senses besides her eyesight. "Don't worry," Finn said reassuringly. "We'll find him."

Rising to her feet, she carried Mikey toward the broken apartment door. He and Abernathy followed close behind. There were dozens of nosy neighbors peeking out of their doorways as he escorted Eva and Mikey outside to his double-parked police-issued SUV. He put Abernathy in the back first, then came around to help Eva.

"I'm sorry," he said, opening the back passenger door open for her. "I shouldn't have yelled."

"Yelling is bad," Mikey said, having calmed down from his scare. "Mommy and Daddy aren't supposed to yell, either. But sometimes they do."

Eva's gaze clashed with his and he gave a brief nod. "Do you know what they were fighting about, Mikey?"

"Mommy spends too much money." Mikey yawned widely, his eyelids drooping as the events of the evening caught up with him. "Daddy said so."

"It's okay, Mikey," Eva said. She buckled the boy into his car seat and then kissed him. "Grown-ups sometimes yell, but you should know that both your mommy and your daddy love you very much."

"I love them, too." Mikey yawned again, his eyelids fluttering closed. His head slid to one side as he appeared to fall asleep.

Eva closed the back passenger door and moved as if to brush past Finn. He stopped her by gently cupping her shoulders in his hands. "Eva, please don't ever jump into danger like that again. My heart nearly stopped when you rushed in to grab Mikey. When I heard the gunshot, I feared the worst."

She lifted her head to look up at him. "Don't ask me to apologize for saving Mikey's life."

"I know, I get it. But your life is precious, too." He knew those moments when she'd run into harm's way would reverberate in his mind forever. "I can't bear to lose you."

She looked surprised by his admission and that made him grin. Unable to help himself, he pulled her close, his mouth hovering above hers. "I want to kiss you," he whispered.

"I'd like that." The words were barely out of her mouth when he covered her lips with his. Their kiss was soft, chaste at first, then grew intense as he allowed the passion he felt to come through.

"Finn? Oh, uh, sorry. I didn't realize the Gallagher charm was striking again."

The interruption was unwelcome, and he lifted his head regretfully. Reed Branson, one of the K-9 officers who'd gone out to look for Mikey was standing nearby. Finn narrowed his gaze, not happy that Reed had mentioned his so-called charm in front of Eva, and didn't bother to hide the edge to his tone. "What?"

"I wanted to know if you still need me to watch over the Stallings' house." The cheeky grin on Reed's face made Finn inwardly groan. This kiss was going to be talked about throughout the K-9 community, no doubt about it. The guys were merciless with their teasing, especially on the basketball court during their informal pickup games. At one time, he'd earned his reputation for dating women with a friendly, no-strings-attached approach. He didn't want Eva to know that.

The feelings he had toward her were different. More intense. More—*everything*.

"Yes. I'm driving them home now, so if you'd follow us that would be great." He opened the passenger door for Eva, who quickly slid inside.

"Just driving them home or sneaking another kiss?" Reed teased. Thankfully, Finn had already closed the door, so he hoped Eva hadn't overheard his remark.

"Just follow us," he said in an annoyed tone.

The ride back to Pete's house didn't take long, and Eva called Pete on the way to reassure him that they'd found Mikey safe and sound. Apparently, Pete hadn't been able to get a flight out because of the storm but was still planning to come home early the following morning. Finn offered to carry Mikey inside, but Eva insisted. He escorted them both into the house, waiting until Eva carried Mikey up to bed.

"Everything okay?" Finn asked.

"Pete claims he doesn't blame me, but I'm not sure I believe him," she said with a sigh.

"Knowing Mikey is safe will be all that matters in the end." Although he ached to hold her, he stayed where he was. "I need to go. If you need anything, Reed Branson will be outside. I want you to feel safe here, okay?"

"Will Reed stay all night?"

"Just till I get back. Since Pete's flight was delayed, I, uh, plan to sleep on the sofa down here in the living room, if that's okay with you."

Eva nodded. "I would feel better having someone here all night, thanks."

Finn wanted desperately to kiss her again but forced himself to leave. Interrogating their perp had to be his top priority.

Down at the local police station, the man they'd arrested for kidnapping Mikey sat in an interrogation room with his wrists handcuffed to the table, his expression defiant. When Finn walked toward the room, he was stopped by the officer who'd transported the man and handed him a folder of information.

"His name is Roger 'Roach' Talmadge," the officer informed him. "Nice nickname, huh? He has a rap sheet mostly related to selling drugs, although there is an aggravated assault on file. More recently, he was a suspect in the airport drug-running operation that Zach investigated. Unfortunately, Roach slipped under the radar and disappeared. Until now. Zach said to go ahead and start the questioning without waiting for him."

"Sounds good to me." Finn took the folder into the interrogation room. "So, Roach, why don't you tell me what's in the package you're so desperate to find?"

Roach stared at him with flat eyes.

Finn tapped the file folder with one finger. "You might want to consider cooperating with us because, with your history, you're looking at hard time. One kidnapping and one attempted kidnaping, both felony convictions. Not to mention aggravated assault and dognapping. You can wait for your lawyer, or you can do yourself a favor and tell us what's going on."

"Not till I speak to my lawyer," Roach said in his raspy voice.

Finn knew what the guy wanted, and that was to cut some sort of deal. The very thought of this jerk getting less prison time because of snitching on his pals made him sick to his stomach, but that was the way the criminal justice system worked. As much as he wanted to shake the truth out of the guy, he knew that there was nothing more they could do until he met with his lawyer.

Frustrated and exhausted, Finn called Zach to let him know Roach wasn't talking, then left the police station to return to Pete's house. Mikey was safe, which was the most important thing. Still, it galled him that they were still no closer to finding out the truth about what was really going on. Or finding Cocoa.

Although patience wasn't one of his strengths, he had no choice but to practice it now. Leaning on God's strength helped, but he wouldn't be satisfied until they had some answers.

The stinky guy with the Southern twang in his voice was still out there somewhere. Finn needed to find him before he could believe Eva and Mikey were safe once and for all.

Eva collapsed on the sofa, her mind reeling with everything that had taken place over the past six hours. Losing Mikey, finding Mikey, calling Pete, kissing Finn.

She'd been caught off guard by Finn's kiss, especially the sweet way he'd asked her permission. No man had ever done that before. What was even more shocking was that Finn had initiated their kiss despite knowing about her retinitis pigmentosa. She'd been honest with him when she'd informed him of what her diagnosis meant—that she'd be declared legally blind in a few years.

Didn't he realize the impact it would have on her life?

Or was it possible the kiss didn't mean as much to him as it had to her? Maybe this was how he treated all the women in his life. What had that other cop said? Something about the Gallagher charm striking again? It wasn't a stretch to believe that Finn was a "date 'em and dump 'em" kind of guy.

Her cheeks burned with embarrassment, and she covered them with the palms of her hands.

Finn might have initiated the kiss because he was accustomed to kissing women, but she'd been a willing participant, agreeing to the kiss and then losing herself in his embrace.

That it meant more to her than it likely had to him shouldn't be a surprise. What man would willingly sign up for dating a woman who'd end up blind? Rafe, the man who'd claimed to love her, had quickly moved on after learning the truth.

Exhaustion weighed her down, but Eva knew she wouldn't be able to rest until Finn was back. How was that for being messed up? The man she shouldn't have kissed was the only man who made her feel safe. Reed Branson, who was keeping watch, was probably a fine cop, but she didn't know him.

Not the way she knew Finn, and believed that the K-9 cop and his partner, Abernathy, would put their lives on the line for her and the little boy sleeping upstairs.

As if on cue, Mikey began to cry. "Mommy. *Mommy!*"

His shriek had her rushing upstairs. She'd left a night-light on for him and could see he was sitting upright in bed, tears streaking down his face. She knelt on the mattress and pulled him close. "Shh, Mikey, it's okay. You're safe. I'm here. We're all safe."

"The bad man is here." He sobbed, a wild

look in his eyes. "We have to hide. The bad man is here."

The words were eerily similar to the day Mikey had been playing with the dinosaurs, claiming the bad man was real because his mommy said so.

Was this a nightmare from the recent events? Or something that had happened in the past?

"Mikey, I'm here, and I love you. You're safe. Officer Finn will be here soon with Abernathy. You love Abe, don't you?"

Mikey nodded, and he repeated, "We have to hide from the bad man. Hurry!"

Eva cuddled him close and chose her words carefully. "Why, Mikey? Because Mommy said so?"

The little boy nodded. "The bad man came to the door. She told me to hide, so I went into the closet. I'm scared. I don't want the bad man to get me again."

A chill snaked down her spine as the implication of his words sank deep. Mikey's recent bad man might have been the same one her sister had told him to hide from in the past. Was that why the two events had been linked in the little boy's mind?

It made sense that if Malina had stolen something from the men, they'd come to confront her. She wished she knew when this hiding incident had happened.

If it had happened at all.

"Mikey, Officer Finn has arrested the bad man who took you," she said, rubbing her hand on his back. "We're safe. The bad man is in jail and can't hurt us anymore."

Mikey buried close, his little body still trembling with fear. "I miss my mommy," he whispered.

Tears filled her eyes. "I know, sweetie. I miss her, too."

She held Mikey close until the little boy went lax against her, falling back asleep. She didn't want to leave him, worried he'd be plagued by nightmares again.

When she heard noises coming from downstairs, she realized Finn was back. Moving carefully, she gently placed the child back onto the mattress and pulled the sheet up to cover his shoulders. She kissed the top of his head, then eased off the mattress, hoping to not wake him.

Finn waited for her at the bottom of the stairs, his gaze full of concern. "Everything all right?"

She shook her head slowly. "Mikey had a nightmare, and I think events from the past are mushed together in his mind with everything that happened tonight."

"What do you mean?"

She repeated what Mikey had told her about hiding in the closet from the bad man because his mother told him to. "I'm thinking he meant the closet in the playroom," she added. "It's actually meant to be a third bedroom." She hated the idea that her sister had exposed the little boy to danger. "I wish we could find that stupid package."

"We searched that closet already," Finn reminded her. "Eddie, Zach's drug-sniffing K-9, didn't alert in there."

"I know." She let out a heavy sigh. "Did you learn anything more?"

"Unfortunately, no. Perp's name is Roger Talmadge, but he won't deal until he's talked to his lawyer."

"Deal?" She stared at him in horror. "Surely he'll pay for what he's done."

"Yes, he will." Finn took her arm and drew her into the living room. "Trust me, he'll go to jail. But we still need to find Cocoa. Not to mention Roach's accomplice."

"You're right." Her knees felt wobbly so she sank onto the sofa. "I understand, truly, but it's just horrible the way Mikey is the one suffering in all of this."

"And you, too," Finn added, his gaze dark with concern. "Don't forget, you were assaulted three times and almost kidnapped. You're in danger, probably more than Mikey. Their next attempt will likely be on you."

She wasn't nearly as worried about herself as she was the innocent little boy sleeping upstairs. "Maybe, but that doesn't matter."

"Yes," Finn said forcefully. "It does."

Touched by his concern, she met his fierce gaze. The kiss they'd shared a short time ago shimmered in the air between them. When it looked as though he might kiss her again, she forced herself to stand, putting distance between them.

"What's wrong?" Finn asked.

"You. Me. This." She waved an exasperated hand between them. "Us. Surely you understand there can't be anything between us."

"If this is about Reed Branson's big mouth," Finn began, but she cut him off.

"It's not." Well, maybe it was a little, but that wasn't the point. "You don't realize what my future holds, Finn, but I do. My eyesight is okay now, not great with my limited peripheral vision, yet I can still see. As the next few years go by, that will change dramatically. My vision will narrow further until I'll only be able to see through a small pinhole, darkness and light, shadows and shapes, and nothing else." She squared her shoulders, facing him. "I won't be treated as an invalid. I train guide dogs for a living and plan to continue doing so even after I lose my eyesight. Don't underestimate my determination to remain independent."

"Okay, I won't." Finn took a step closer, drilling her with his intense gaze. "If you promise to do the same."

She frowned. "What do you mean?"

He came closer and stole a quick kiss before stepping back. "I won't underestimate you if you don't underestimate me."

She gasped in surprise, not sure what to make of that. Finn didn't move, so she finally turned away. "I need to get some sleep. Good night, Finn."

"Good night."

As she headed upstairs, Eva replayed their conversation in her mind. Was he serious? Was it possible that she could have the future she'd always dreamed of?

A husband and family of her own.

ELEVEN

Finn was able to catch a few hours of sleep, but woke early, anxious to continue working the case. After taking Abernathy outside and giving his K-9 partner fresh water and food, he sat down at the kitchen table to make notes. He'd already sent two samples of cocaine to the lab, and needed to check if Ilana Hawkins, their forensic lab tech, had any updates on the cocaine matching, the fingerprints from the paper-wrapped rock or the DNA from Eva's keys, and finally, there was the interview with Roach. The last issue was the one where he had the greatest hope of getting something to crack this case. Guys like Roach were always willing to make a deal in exchange for a lighter sentence.

When he heard movement from upstairs, he headed into the kitchen to make coffee and start breakfast. He knew, deep in his bones, that Eva was the primary person in danger now. Mikey was safe, and he didn't think there'd be another attempt on the child, not when they'd been able to find him so quickly. Yet Finn understood that until the missing package was recovered and the stinky guy with a twang had been captured, they had to be extremely careful.

"Good morning." Eva's husky voice had him turning toward the doorway. His breath caught in his chest at how beautiful she was, even after just waking up and without a bit of makeup. Her natural beauty needed no enhancements. The kiss they'd shared flashed into his mind, and he wished he had the right to greet her with a kiss.

She'd drawn a line in the sand last night, one he couldn't bring himself to cross.

"Morning." Had that croaky voice come from him? He cleared his throat, noticing Mikey scampering over to pet Abernathy, and tried again. "I'm making pancakes for breakfast if you're hungry."

"I'm very hungry," Mikey said. The little boy gave Abernathy one last pat, then turned toward Finn, raising his arms in a way that silently indicated he wanted to be lifted up.

Finn obliged him by hauling the boy into his arms. The child wrapped his arms around his neck, resting his head on Finn's shoulder.

"I miss my daddy."

Finn's gaze clashed with Eva's, catching the hint of tears shimmering in her eyes. "I know, buddy. He'll be home soon." He rubbed the boy's back reassuringly before setting Mikey into his booster seat.

"Thanks for making breakfast." Eva brushed past him, and her citrusy scent made him forget what he was about to say.

"Uh…" He glanced around the kitchen, then remembered. "Oh, I have fresh coffee here if you're interested."

"I'd love some." She looked tired, and he wondered if Mikey had suffered more nightmares during the night. He hadn't heard crying but knew that didn't mean the child hadn't woken her up.

He poured a mug of coffee and pulled milk out of the fridge for her, too, knowing she preferred it that way. Turning back to the stove, he flipped the pancakes and then glanced at her.

"You're staying here with Mikey today."

She nodded. "With police guarding the house, right?"

"Yes. Any idea when Pete is getting in?"

"Not sure. He was hoping to get the first flight out of Atlanta."

After watching the pancakes for another minute, he flipped them off the griddle and onto a plate. He set them on the table, then chose a seat between Mikey and Eva. "Let's pray."

"Pray?" Mikey echoed with confusion.

Finn took the boy's hand and then held out

his other hand toward Eva. She placed her small palm in his. "Yes, we need to pray before we eat."

"But I'm hungry," Mikey insisted.

"This will only take a minute." Finn bent his head. "Dear Lord, we thank You for this food we are about to eat. We also thank You for keeping Mikey safe in Your care and for providing us the strength to find him. We ask that You continue to guide us on Your chosen path. Amen."

"Amen," Eva said, her voice clear and firm.

Finn glanced at Mikey. "You need to say 'Amen,' too," he encouraged.

"Amen," Mikey repeated. "Now can I eat?"

Finn chuckled and released the boy's hand. "Yes, now you can eat." He glanced at Eva and winked before releasing her hand.

She blushed. He found himself hoping that meant she was remembering their kiss and that soon the line she'd drawn would be wiped away. She avoided his gaze, taking a deep sip of her coffee.

Pulling himself together, he helped cut up Mikey's pancakes and added a nice dollop of maple syrup. "I have to report in to work," he told her. "There will be two officers in a squad car parked out front, keeping an eye on the place while I'm gone. I'll head back here as soon as possible."

"I appreciate that." She helped herself to a pancake. "Hmm. This is delicious."

"See? Told you I could cook," he teased.

She blushed again, and his heart squeezed in his chest. This wasn't good. He was getting far too emotionally attached to Eva. He forced himself to remember how his own mother couldn't handle being a cop's wife. How he'd been determined not to make the same mistake his father had.

He finished his breakfast quickly, then rose to carry his empty plate to the sink. "I'm sorry to leave you with the dishes, but I have to go."

"It's not a problem," Eva insisted. "I need to clean the place up before Pete gets home anyway."

Finn hesitated, then nodded. "Come, Abernathy."

The yellow Lab came instantly to his side. Finn leaned over to rub his silky fur, then clipped on Abernathy's vest and leash. He tucked the food and water dishes under his arm. "Call if you need something."

"Okay. Let me know if you find anything."

"I will." Finn went over to press a kiss on the top of Mikey's head. "See you later, buddy. Be good for your aunt Eva."

"I will." Mikey grinned, his face sticky with syrup.

The domestic scene was becoming a bit much, so Finn quickly left with Abernathy. It pained him to realize how much he suddenly wanted what he'd told himself he could never have.

A family.

* * *

Eva called Wade to let him know she wouldn't be at work that day. Her boss was uncharacteristically upset with her decision.

"Eva, with Cocoa missing, it's even more important that you work with George. He needs to have the basics in place so he's ready to be fostered."

"Finn is going to find Cocoa." She truly believed in Finn and Abernathy. "And it's only for one more day. Pete should be home later this afternoon."

"Listen, Eva, I need your full attention on training these pups. I have owners who have paid a lot of money for guide dogs and they're expecting results."

"I know, I know." She didn't understand why Wade was getting upset over one additional day off. "I'll be in tomorrow," she repeated. Without giving Wade time to argue, she disconnected from the line. She understood this was all getting to her boss, but she was under even more stress than he was. Normally he didn't mind when she adjusted her schedule as needed.

She hoped the guide dog training center wasn't having financial difficulties. She decided to ask Wade about it tomorrow when she reported in for work.

By late morning, Mikey was getting bored.

"I wanna go to preschool," he whined. "I miss my friends."

"Not today," she said, glancing at her watch. How she'd keep Mikey occupied indoors for the rest of the day was beyond her. The rain from yesterday had moved on, leaving bright sunlight behind. "Tell you what? I'll see if Officer Finn will take us to get your Father's Day finger painting framed when he's finished with work. How does that sound?"

The boy nodded eagerly. "Okay."

Before she could call Finn, her phone rang. She answered immediately when she noticed Pete's name on the screen. "Hi. Are you on your way home?"

"Just getting on a flight in the next thirty minutes," her brother-in-law responded. "The earlier flight was overbooked, so I had to wait until this one that's scheduled to go out at noon. The storm messed up a lot of flights, so I'm stuck with a layover in Chicago. I probably won't get in until well after dinnertime." There was a pause, then Pete asked, "How is Mikey?"

"He's fine. Truly. I kept him home from preschool and we have a cop stationed outside. We're safe, don't worry. Do you want to talk to him?"

"Yeah." Pete sounded choked up, and she could only imagine how difficult it must have been for him to be in stuck in Atlanta while knowing his son had been kidnapped.

"Mikey, say hi to your daddy." She turned the phone so that the little boy could see his father's face.

"Hi, Daddy!" Mikey waved at his father. "Are you coming home soon?"

"Yes, Mikey. Very soon. I'll be there before you go to bed tonight."

"I have a surprise for you," Mikey said eagerly.

"Don't tell him," Eva cautioned. "Remember? It's a secret for Father's Day."

"I can't wait to see your surprise, Mikey." Pete's voice grew husky. "I love you and will see you soon, okay?"

"Okay. Bye, Daddy!" Mikey waved again, and this time Eva could see Pete's eyes were moist.

"Bye, son. I'll call you when I land, Eva," Pete added.

"I'll talk to you then." She disconnected from the call, knowing that once Pete returned she'd have to go back to her place. After the rock incident, she'd convinced her friends to stay at a hotel for a couple of nights.

She could stay at a hotel, too, but didn't like being in a strange place overnight. Her night vision wasn't great, and she always ended up walking into furniture in the dark. She preferred being at home, among her own things and where she was familiar with the layout of each and every room.

Something to worry about later. She called

Finn, but he didn't answer. She left a quick message related to Mikey's request to get his painting framed, then chastised herself for bothering Finn while he was at work.

This attachment she'd formed with Finn couldn't go anywhere. She knew it. He knew it. They might be attracted to each other, but that didn't mean they needed to do anything about it.

Once they'd arrested the stinky guy with the Southern twang and got Cocoa back, she wouldn't be seeing Finn any longer.

And that was exactly the way it should be.

Finn spent the morning getting caught up. He focused on writing up his report of Mikey's kidnapping and subsequent rescue, a task that took longer than he'd anticipated. When he finished with that, he followed up on the other outstanding issues. The news related to the paper-covered rock that had sailed through Eva's window wasn't good. No fingerprints, nothing unusual about the paper or the color printer the photo had been printed from.

In other words, a dead end.

The lab didn't have any DNA results back yet but was still checking the two cocaine samples to see if they were similar. Cocaine was often cut by other substances to dilute the drug, enabling the dealer to make more money. If the chemical composition of the two samples was exactly the same, it was likely they'd both come from the same batch. What that meant wasn't clear, but he intended to cover every possible angle.

"Noah, I'm heading over to interview Roger Talmadge, aka Roach." He glanced at Noah Jameson, who had recently been named the interim chief, filling his brother Jordan's role in the wake of his murder, which had been staged to look like a suicide. Finn and the rest of the close-knit K-9 team did not for one minute believe their former chief killed himself. It bothered Finn that he hadn't been able to get much done on Jordan's case, and he made a silent promise to work on it later that afternoon. Once he'd got whatever information he could squeeze out of Roach.

"Don't bother," Zach Jameson said, walking toward him. "His lawyer has been delayed in court, so he's still not talking."

Finn let out an exasperated breath. "Great. Now what?"

"Now we wait." Zach shrugged.

"Not happening." Finn dragged his hands through his hair. "I'm going over the list of known associates again. One of them has to be the stinky guy with the Southern twang."

"The stinky guy with the Southern twang?" Zach raised a brow.

"That's how Eva describes him." He abruptly remembered what Eva had mentioned last night. "Stinky with sweat, right? Maybe they originally met at the gym Malina used to go to. The Fitness Club." He could barely contain his excitement. He'd planned on checking out the gym for the package anyway, but the idea that the stinky guy might have used the place as well only cemented the connection. "Come, Abernathy."

"You need backup?" Zach asked.

He was about to refuse, then realized that Eddie's drug-sniffing nose might come in handy. "Yeah, in fact, I think we need to check the place out, see if we can find any hint of drugs there."

"We should get a search warrant," Zach pointed out.

Finn hesitated, then nodded. "You're right. I'll write up the paper on that while you find a judge who will grant it."

Writing up the request and finding a judge to sign off took another hour, and then they had exactly what they needed to access Malina's locker—if she had one—at The Fitness Club.

They took separate cars because the K-9s needed to be safely transported in their own spaces. When they arrived at The Fitness Club, Finn and Zach led their respective dogs inside. Their agreement was that Finn would take the lead on asking questions and providing the warrant while Eddie searched the main area for the scent of drugs.

"I'm K-9 Officer Finn Gallagher and this is my search-and-rescue partner, Abernathy. I'd like to know if Malina Stallings had a membership here?"

"Uh, do you have a warrant?" The woman behind the desk had a name tag that identified her as Yasmine.

"Yes." He handed her the paperwork.

"I need to call my boss," Yasmine said. "This is above my pay grade."

"No need to call your boss. Just tell us if Malina had a locker here. She died in a car crash that was deemed accidental, but I'm formally requesting to reopen the case. I believe she was murdered. If there's no locker, then there's nothing for us to search, right?"

"Oh, she's the victim of a crime?" Yasmin's expression softened. "That's horrible. Let's see what I have on file." She tapped a few keys and then glanced up. "Yes, Malina Stallings has a membership here."

"A current one?" Finn tried to keep the surprise out of his tone.

"Yes. Her membership is paid through June. She prepaid for six months."

That was interesting and made him doubt Pete's claims of innocence once again. "And what about a locker?"

"Yes, she paid for that, as well. Locker number twenty-six." Yasmine glanced between Finn and Zach. "But it's in the ladies' locker room, and I think it would be best if I called my boss before I let you search the locker."

"This warrant gives us permission, regardless of your boss says," Finn pointed out. "You can either help us out, or we'll just go back there on our own. Your choice."

Yasmine looked indecisive for a moment, then shrugged. "Okay. I'll get the master key and make sure the locker room is empty so you can go in."

"Thanks for your cooperation, Yasmine." Finn waited until she went to clear the locker room before glancing at Zach. "Eddie pick up anything?"

"Negative."

"The contents of the locker might be exactly what we're looking for," Finn said in a low voice.

"I hope so," Zach agreed.

"It's all clear," Yasmine announced. She held the locker-room door open and handed Finn a key. "I'll keep everyone out until you're finished."

"Thanks." He and Zach took their respective K-9s inside the women's locker room. They found locker twenty-six without trouble, and Finn could feel his heart pounding in his chest as he opened the locker door.

But all he found were sweaty clothes, a bag of makeup and other toiletries. No package.

"Hey, what's this?" Zach put his pinky finger against some white powder clinging to the corner of the locker.

Eddie alerted on the scent and Finn nodded

grimly. "We'll bag that as evidence, too, and compare it to the other samples."

"Will do."

The trace of cocaine wasn't what he'd been hoping for; yet, knowing Malina had kept her gym membership was an interesting tidbit of information.

Unfortunately, they didn't have any way to link Eva's stinky guy to the gym. Finn began to despair they'd ever find Cocoa.

Or the man searching so desperately for the missing package.

TWELVE

Eva told herself to stop staring at her phone, waiting for Finn to return her call. He was busy working the case, which was the most important thing right now. Not getting Mikey's finger painting framed.

When her phone rang, she pounced on it. Disappointment washed over her when she saw Pete's name on the screen. "Hi, how was your flight?"

"I'm in Chicago, but there's an engine problem with the plane so we have to wait for a replacement." Sharp frustration laced his tone. "It's as if everything is working against me this trip."

"I'm sorry, Pete, but please know that things here are fine." She found herself wishing Pete might find some solace in prayer, but she didn't say anything. She was too new to the idea of praying. "I haven't let Mikey out of my sight and we still have a squad car sitting in the driveway."

"Yeah, I know." Pete sighed heavily. "It's just that I need to be there, to hold Mikey close. I never should have left him—" He broke off what he was about to say, but Eva could easily fill in the blank.

"With me," she said.

"That's not what I meant," Pete interjected, backpedaling.

"No, it's okay. I'd probably feel the same way if our situation was reversed. And Mikey was taken right under my nose. I never should have turned my back on him, even for a second."

"Don't, Eva, please?" The pent-up frustration left Pete's tone. "If you blame yourself, then I have to take my share, too. This is all related to Malina stealing some package, which makes me culpable. I should have known something was seriously wrong between us. Should have figured out she might be involved in something criminal. The way she was going through money…" He didn't finish his thought.

"We were both close to Malina," Eva pointed out. "How about we stop playing the blame game and do our best to move forward from here?"

"I'll try." There was a pause before he added, "I'll text you when we finally have a plane so you can figure out when my flight might get in."

"Okay, see you later, then."

Eva set her phone aside and went to the playroom to check on Mikey. He was curled up in a beanbag chair, his eyes drooping as a Disney movie played on the television. She knew the little boy hadn't got much sleep last night between bouts of nightmares, so she left him alone, returning to the kitchen.

She'd taken a package of chicken breasts out of the freezer, determined to make at least one home-cooked meal for her nephew. She found one of Malina's recipes for a cheesy chicken and veggies dish that looked easy enough.

Finn returned her call a few minutes later. "Hey, I'm getting ready to leave headquarters. I should be there within twenty minutes or so, and we can leave for the custom-framing craft shop whenever it's convenient for you."

She was glad Finn wasn't there to see the silly smile that had bloomed on her face. "Mikey's taking a nap now, but I don't expect him to sleep for long. Oh, and I'm cooking dinner—nothing fancy, but hopefully edible. You're welcome to join us."

"I'd love to." Her silly smile widened at his words. "See you soon."

"Bye." Once again, she set her phone aside, then turned toward the food items she had sitting on the counter. Determined to prove she wasn't a complete imbecile in the kitchen, she painstakingly followed the recipe and then set the covered dish in the fridge so she could bake it in the oven later.

"Auntie Eva, I'm hungry." Mikey's plaintive tone had her moving quickly to the playroom.

She scooped the boy into her arms and kissed his cheek.

"How about a snack while we wait for Officer Finn?"

Mikey perked up. "We're going to get my picture framed for Daddy?"

"Yes, we are." After all the excitement from the night before, having normal plans for the evening seemed strange. There was a small part of her that feared leaving the house, but she shrugged it off. Finn wouldn't let either of them out of his sight, and they'd have Abernathy with them, too. "We'll do that first, then when we get back home we'll have dinner."

Mikey nodded. "Pizza?"

"No, I'm making dinner tonight, one of your mommy's recipes."

Mikey's lower lip trembled, and she instantly wished she hadn't mentioned his mother.

"It's okay, Mikey. Your mommy is here, in your heart." She tapped his chest lightly. "She'll always love you."

Mikey patted his chest, too, following her lead. "Is my daddy coming home? Or is he in my heart, too?"

"Oh, sweetie." Her heart ached for the little boy. "Your daddy is in your heart, but he'll also be home tonight, hopefully before you go to bed. But even if he can't get home until later, he'll give you a hug and a kiss when he arrives, okay?"

"Okay." Mikey seemed mollified by that, and she let out a soundless sigh, feeling good that the impending crisis had been adverted. For now.

She gave Mikey animal crackers and milk for his snack and put the finger painting off to the side of the table, in case of a spill. Finn arrived ahead of schedule, Eva greeted him with a warm smile.

"You made good time."

"I did." Finn took a moment to fill Abernathy's water dish, then came over to ruffle Mikey's hair. "Hey, buddy. Ready to head out to get your picture framed?"

"Yes!" Mikey's tone was full of excitement.

"All right, then. If you're finished with your snack, we can leave."

"Goody!" Mikey squirmed out of his booster seat and the three of them, along with Abernathy, went outside.

The drive to the craft store took longer than picking out a frame. While they waited in the checkout line with the finished product, an older woman smiled at them. "Oh, look at that, your son made a family portrait! How sweet."

Eva smiled and nodded, not bothering to correct the woman's assumption that Mikey's drawing was of the three of them. But when Finn glanced at her and winked, she blushed.

Finn's carefree attitude confused her. His playfulness was helpful during times of stress, and at other times, like now, it seemed to be his way of telling her not to take this—whatever it was between them—too seriously.

Just another reminder of how she needed to protect herself from becoming emotionally attached.

Finn loved the way Eva blushed and had to stop himself from stealing a kiss right there in the middle of the store. The framed finger painting turned out better than he'd expected, and he hoped Pete Stallings knew how fortunate he was to have a son like Mikey.

Despite digging deep into Pete's background, he hadn't found anything suspicious. That fact didn't preclude Stallings from being guilty, but proving the guy was involved in his wife's death or with drug dealing in general would be impossible without some hard evidence.

When Eva had told him about Pete being delayed in Chicago, his doubt around the guy's innocence in this mess had grown exponentially. One man couldn't have that much trouble flying home from a trip, could he? Sure, anything was possible, but Finn wasn't buying it. Not yet. Not until they knew for certain who was behind the attempts against Eva and Mikey.

Maybe once Pete was back in Queens, he'd slip up somehow, giving Finn and his K-9 team the proof they needed.

Stallings wasn't the only lead he was following up on. The Fitness Club was another angle. He couldn't dismiss the possibility that Eva's stinky guy was also a member and maybe even had met Malina there. Finding the cocaine in her locker wasn't a total surprise, but he'd really hoped to have found the missing package, even though he knew the stinky guy might have already tried to search there for it. If he could find a way into the women's locker room without being seen.

The longer it took to find the package, the more convinced he was that there was no package to find. Malina had already used the drugs or the money for herself.

"Finn? We're ready."

Eva's voice broke into his thoughts. He glanced over in surprise to see her holding Mikey on her hip and the framed picture under her arm. He'd followed them through the checkout line, but he'd been so lost in thought he hadn't realized Eva had finished up at checkout.

"Sorry, here, let me carry that for you." He took the picture from her and led the way outside. They had to walk a few blocks to his SUV, and he made sure to keep an eye out for any sign of danger as they did so. His gaze landed on a black four-door sedan, but it disappeared from view before he could catch a glimpse of the driver. Was the stinky guy following them? The possibility was like a fist squeezing his heart.

No way was he going to allow anything to happen to Mikey. Or to Eva.

He opened the back of his white SUV for Abernathy and then tucked the framed painting on the floor. Eva buckled Mikey into his car seat.

The ride back to Pete's house was filled with Mikey's chatter. Eva carried Mikey inside, leaving Finn to follow with Abernathy and the framed picture.

"It will just take me a minute to pop this into the oven," she said in the kitchen, pulling a shallow baking pan from the fridge. "Dinner will be ready soon. Oh, and would you mind helping me wrap this for Mikey and Pete?"

"I don't mind at all. Give me a minute to take care of my partner." He noticed Abernathy standing at the door, looking over at him as if to say, *What's taking so long?*

"Coming," he said, talking to Abernathy as he always did. Some might think he was weird for talking to his dog. For a long time it had just been him and Abernathy. Until he'd met Eva.

Now all he could think about was her. Seeing her. Kissing her. Spending time with her.

If he didn't watch out, he'd fall in love with her.

The notion of being in love was something he'd never really believed in. His parents hadn't been shining examples of everlasting love. And while he'd watched a few his colleagues claim to be in love, he wasn't sure how they knew their feelings were real or whether those feelings would survive the bad times, despite the wedding vows that claimed otherwise.

All women weren't like his mother. But he also knew that cops had the highest divorce rate of any profession. Not just because of the unpredictable nature of the job, but also because cops witnessed firsthand the horrific things people could do to each other.

Often, a case took a piece of a cop's heart, until there was nothing left for himself, much less his family.

When Abernathy finished with his nature call, Finn cleaned up the mess and went back inside. He left Abernathy with Mikey and went into the bathroom to wash up.

"Dinner will be ready in thirty minutes," Eva said when he walked into the kitchen. The way she twisted her hands together betrayed her nervousness. "I used Malina's recipe, so there's no reason it shouldn't turn out."

"I'm sure it will be delicious," he assured her. "Now, where's that wrapping paper?"

It was a good thing nobody was there to critique their wrapping job, because it left a lot to be desired. His fingers tangled with Eva's more than once, and they both ended up with tape and bits of paper stuck to their skin.

Listening to Eva laughing at the final product made Finn realize how little she'd had to laugh about in the past few days. Since the day he'd met her, she'd faced one struggle after another.

He made a silent promise to work harder at bringing her joy.

The atmosphere in the kitchen was homey as he cleaned up the mess on the table and Eva took the cheesy chicken out of the oven.

"Mikey, time for dinner," Finn called. "Abernathy, come."

His K-9 partner came into the kitchen with Mikey, grabbing at the dog's tail, hot on his heels. "Don't hurt Abe," Finn warned.

"I won't. I love Abe." As if to prove it, Mikey put his arms around the animal's neck and gave him a kiss. Abernathy licked him in response.

"Up you go." Finn lifted Mikey into his booster seat. "Don't forget we have to pray," he told the child.

"I won't forget." Mikey leaned over to see the dog, who'd taken up his usual position as sentry on duty beside Mikey's chair. Abernathy was too well trained to beg, but he wasn't going to allow any food to hit the floor for long, either.

In a matter of minutes the table was set and the steamy cheesy chicken bake was in the center of the table.

"This time, I'd like to say grace," Eva said as she took her seat beside Finn.

"Of course," he agreed, pleased she'd taken the lead. He took her hand in his and then grasped

Mikey's hand. To his surprise, Mikey reached down to put his other hand on Abernathy's head, as if including his partner in their prayer.

"Dear Lord, thanks for keeping Mikey safe. Please help Finn and the other officers working the case find the men responsible for their crimes. Please continue to keep us safe. Amen."

"Amen," Finn echoed.

"And Abe, too," Mikey added. "Amen."

That made Finn laugh, and he was grateful that Eva smiled, as well. Mission accomplished, he thought.

He helped cut up Mikey's food and then took a bite. "Yum, this is fantastic."

Eva blushed again and shook her head. "It's Malina's recipe, not mine."

"Better than takeout any day." He didn't like the way she put herself down and made a mental note to talk about that later. Her phone chirped and he glanced at her expectantly.

"Pete texted me that he's on the plane heading home," she said and set the phone aside. "He probably won't land here until nine o'clock, though."

"I can pick him up at the airport," he offered, thinking it might be a good time to question the guy about his relationship with Malina and the missing package.

"Oh, no, that's too much of a bother. Pete told me he'll call a car service."

"Okay." Finn figured he'd wait here for Pete to get home and talk to him then. "I may stick around for a while if you don't mind. I have some computer work to take care of."

"Fine with me."

After finishing their dinner, Finn helped clear the table while Eva took care of Mikey. It was beyond Finn how the kid always managed to get food in his hair, but Eva didn't seem to mind taking him upstairs to give him a bath.

Abernathy licked his chops and sniffed along the floor as if looking for any spare crumb he might have missed. Once Finn had the dishes taken care of, he took Abernathy outside again, looking around to make sure the house wasn't being watched by anyone nearby. Thankfully, there was no sign of the black sedan. Finn grabbed his laptop from the SUV and carried it inside.

He set up a makeshift office along one side of the kitchen table. Listening to Eva and Mikey with one ear, he booted up the laptop and began organizing his notes.

If the three separate cocaine samples from the upstairs bathroom, Malina's locker and the apartment Roach was using all matched, that would mean the cocaine had come from the same batch. How could he use that to their advantage? He listed off the questions as they popped into his head.

Had Malina worked for Roach? What was her job? To sell the drugs or to simply transport them from one place to another? Was she involved in handling the cash inflows? Why had she taken the package from Roach and his accomplice? For personal use? Or to sell on her own? Had she really thought she could get away with doing something like that without repercussions?

He stared at the list of questions, thinking about how Malina had got fired from the guide dog training center yet had maintained her Fitness Club gym membership. What other secrets had she kept hidden from those closest to her? Remembering the five hundred dollars Eva had found in Malina's bag, he couldn't help but believe there had been many.

But the real question revolved around motive. Why would Malina get involved with these guys in the first place? She had a husband, a beautiful son, a job at the guide dog training center. Why risk it all?

He turned his attention to the list of patrons that had been provided by the woman behind the desk at The Fitness Club. He'd had to fax in a court order for the list and she'd immediately sent it to him.

Scanning the names of gym members was depressing. There were so many of them, and even if he split the list in half, he had over 250 men's names to sift through.

Frustrated, he closed the document as Eva entered the kitchen. "Something wrong?"

"Other than that I'm sitting here spinning my wheels on this case? Not at all."

"No new evidence today?"

He hesitated, not sure he should be confiding in her. Sure, Eva was a victim in this crime, but it was an ongoing and active investigation. She deserved to know the truth, but he wasn't so certain his boss would agree. "Not really."

"I thought Roach wanted to make a deal?"

"He will, but his lawyer was tied up today and the DA's office wants to be involved, so we aren't set up to meet until tomorrow."

"Bummer." Eva sighed and then yawned. "Oops. Sorry. I guess my lack of sleep is catching up to me."

He longed to take her into his arms but forced himself to stay where he was. This attraction he felt toward her was getting out of control. Maybe it was time to pack up and head home. Pete would be here in an hour or so and he had a cop stationed outside the house. There was really no reason to stay here with Eva like this.

Mikey and Abernathy came running into the room. "Can Abe sleep with me tonight? Please?" Mikey looked squeaky-clean in his Superman pajamas.

"Oh, I'm not sure that's allowed," Eva said, responding before he had a chance. "Abe is a police dog, not a pet."

"But I wanna sleep with Abe so I won't be scared." The little boy's clear blue eyes were wide and pleading.

"You can sleep with Abe for a little while," Finn offered. "Until I need to head home."

"Yay! Thanks, Officer Finn." Mikey ran over and gave Finn a hug. Finn kissed the top of the boy's head, breathing in the comforting scent of baby shampoo.

"You're welcome." He cleared his throat and glanced at Eva. "I won't be in your hair for much longer."

She gave him an odd look and simply nodded. "Come on, Mikey. I'll read you a bedtime story."

The kitchen felt empty after they left, and it occurred to Finn how much he'd grown accustomed to having Eva and Mikey around. Annoyed with himself, he turned his attention back to his work.

As he reviewed the information he'd dug up on The Fitness Club, he stumbled across the name of Grant Ulrich. *Ulrich, Ulrich.*

Why was that name so familiar?

He pulled a thick file from his computer case and began searching through the paperwork he had in there from other drug-related cases. In particular, from the recent drug bust Zach Jameson had uncovered at LaGuardia.

There! He pulled a sheet of paper from the

pack and stabbed the name with his index finger. Grant Ulrich. Not only did he own The Fitness Club but also the furniture store, located near the airport and found to be central to the drug-smuggling operation.

Was The Fitness Club another undercover operation for dealing and smuggling drugs?

THIRTEEN

Eva read Mikey one of his favorite bedtime stories, touched by how the little boy snuggled up against Abernathy. When Mikey finally drifted off to sleep, she set the book aside and watched him for a moment.

Pete would be home soon, putting an end to her babysitting duties. Oh, she'd still help out, especially on the nights he had to work twenty-four hours, but it wouldn't be the same. These past few days had only shown her what her diagnosis was taking from her.

Not just her sight, which was bad enough, but no one would want to risk starting a family with her given the chances of passing retinitis pigmentosa on to her children. Besides, remaining independent even after she'd lost her vision was important. She refused to be a burden to anyone.

Especially not to Finn Gallagher.

So this was it. She'd move on with her life

alone. The best she could do was to continue helping Pete with Mikey as needed.

It would have to be enough.

Easing off the mattress, Eva left Mikey sleeping. Abernathy lifted his head, his tail thumping against the bed. She reached over to pet the dog's silky head, silently encouraging him to stay with the little boy for a while longer.

Abernathy set his head back down on the mattress and closed his eyes. She smiled and took a quick picture with her phone of Mikey and the K-9.

She returned downstairs to find Finn still working on his computer. She dropped into a chair next to him. "Mikey's asleep."

Finn nodded, his gaze searching hers. "I'm sticking around until Pete returns home. I don't want you to be upset, but it's important I ask him a few questions."

"About what?" She frowned, not liking where this was going. "You can't seriously believe that Pete hired Roach and the stinky guy. Why would he?"

"I don't believe anything, but as part of the investigation, I need to rule everyone in or out." His gaze bored into hers. "To rule Pete out once and for all, I need to talk to him. Get more detailed information from him."

She sighed heavily and glanced away. Finn wasn't going to let it go, so there was no point in arguing. "Fine, but the poor guy is going to be exhausted by the time he gets home," Eva said. "You might want to give him a chance to rest up before you begin interrogating him."

"It won't be an interrogation," Finn said in a mild tone. "And the sooner he answers my questions, the sooner he can get back to his normal routine."

A wave of panic hit hard. "You're going to keep a cop stationed here until the stinky guy is caught, right?"

"Yes. Don't worry, Mikey will be safe."

"Good." She put her hand over her heart, willing it to slow down. Those moments when she'd realized Mikey had been kidnapped would be forever etched in her memory.

"What about you?" Finn asked. "Are you staying here tonight?"

"Oh, I don't think that's necessary." The thought of going back to the house she shared with her college roommates wasn't appealing, especially since she'd encouraged them both to stay in a hotel for a few days. Which hadn't gone over well, since Alecia owned the place and hadn't liked being moved out of her home. On the other hand, she couldn't help thinking that Mikey would be safer once she was gone.

"I think it is," Finn countered. "At least for tonight. Tomorrow we'll have a chance to work something out with Roach, and we should have your stinky guy in custody by the end of the day."

She nodded slowly, considering his point. What was one more night? No reason not to sleep on the sofa. "Okay, as long as Pete doesn't mind."

"Why would he?"

She shrugged. "You said yourself that I'm a potential target. By now, the stinky guy must know we've searched the house up and down without finding the stupid package. And he still has Cocoa."

"Yeah, but if the guy was smart, he'd return the puppy and get out of town. He must know we have Roach in custody. Why not save himself?"

His theory made sense. "I hope you're right. I've been praying to get Cocoa back safe and sound."

"I'm glad to hear you're leaning on your faith," Finn said in a low, husky tone.

She ducked her head, hoping he wouldn't notice her blush. "Thanks to you, Finn."

Their gazes caught and held, awareness simmering between them. The kitchen shrank in size, creating a cozy atmosphere as if they were alone in the world.

"Eva?" The way Finn said her name in that deep, husky tone made her shiver. She couldn't tear her gaze from his, and when he slowly stood, her heart thudded wildly with anticipation.

"We shouldn't," she whispered as he drew her to her feet.

"Why not? What's wrong with one kiss?"

The only thing wrong with one kiss was that it made her long for two kisses. Three. And more. Yet she couldn't find the strength to push him away. Finn pulled her close gently, and she willingly wrapped her arms around his neck, drawing him toward her.

"Yes," she whispered as he stared at her for a long moment. "One kiss."

His mouth caressed her lips, and she knew in that moment that one kiss would never be enough. Clinging to Finn's broad shoulders, she reveled in the kiss, memorizing his touch, his taste, his musky aftershave.

The sound of a car door slamming outside startled them both. Instantly Finn lifted his head, reaching for the weapon on his hip with his right hand while pushing her behind him with the other.

She heard the jangle of keys and put her hand on Finn's arm. "It's Pete."

Finn didn't lower his weapon as he cautiously approached the door to peek through the window. Eva ran her fingers through her hair, hoping Pete wouldn't notice what he'd interrupted even as she tried to understand Finn's motive behind the kiss.

Pete's timing was awful, but Finn told himself to get over it. Still, it wasn't easy to focus with his head full of Eva's citrusy scent.

Abernathy appeared next to Finn. The K-9 must have heard the sound of Pete's arrival and had come down from the master bedroom in response.

"Heel," Finn commanded as he holstered his weapon. Abernathy sat on his haunches and looked up at Finn, waiting for the next command. "Stay."

The door swung open, revealing a tall, dark-haired twenty-eight-year-old man standing there. Pete looked surprised to see them as he crossed the threshold.

"What's going on?" Pete demanded. "Did something happen with Mikey since we last spoke?"

"No, everything is fine." Eva's smile didn't quite reach her eyes, and Finn wondered if she thought that Pete held her responsible for Mikey's kidnapping.

"Thanks. It's good to be home." Pete dropped his carry-on duffel bag on the floor and eyed Finn curiously. "And you are?"

"Officer Finn Gallagher. This is my partner, Abernathy." Finn didn't offer his hand as he gestured toward the kitchen table. "Take a seat. I have a few questions, if you don't mind."

Pete frowned and rubbed his hand over his lower jaw. "Now?"

"It won't take long and then I'll be on my way." Finn's tone was firm.

There was a long pause as the two men stared

at each other. Finn could tell Pete wanted to tell him to shove off, but managed to maintain his cool.

"Fine. Give me a minute to check on my son." Pete brushed past Finn on his way toward the staircase leading to the second floor.

"He's in your bedroom," Eva called after him.

Pete raised a hand, indicating he'd heard.

She rounded on Finn, her blue eyes flashing with anger as if the amazing kiss they'd shared hadn't happened. "I told you to give him some time."

"And I need to do my job." He tried not to take her verbal attack personally. As a cop he knew what needed to be done, and if Eva didn't understand that, then maybe their kiss had been a mistake.

An uncomfortable silence hung between them, and he tried to think of a way to ease the tension. He was about to apologize, for what he wasn't sure, when he heard the sound of Pete's footsteps.

"Mikey seems fine," Pete said, his voice husky with emotion. "I owe you both a debt of gratitude for finding him so quickly."

"Oh, Pete." Eva rushed over to give her brother-in-law a quick hug. "Finn and Abernathy get the credit for finding Mikey. I just hope you'll forgive me."

"I told you, it's not your fault." Pete returned her hug awkwardly, patting her back before breaking away to face Finn. He crossed his arms over his chest and asked, "What do you want to know?"

"Please, take a seat." Finn didn't want to conduct his interview under hostile circumstances. When Pete reluctantly sat, Finn took a chair beside him. Eva was on Pete's other side, and again he had to ignore the flash of hurt. "I need to understand what you know about your wife's activities before she died."

"I don't know anything about what she was doing." Pete stared blindly off in the distance. "I guess I should have noticed the signs—her emotions were all over the place. One minute she'd be furious, then a few hours later she'd act happy and full of enthusiasm." Pete shrugged. "It was so bad that I was constantly on guard, never sure which Malina would walk through the door."

"And you don't know anything about a package?" Finn pressed.

"Nothing." Pete spread his hands in a helpless gesture. "Ever since Eva mentioned it, I've been racking my brains trying to figure out if I saw anything that could have been a hidden package."

"Do you have a safe-deposit box?"

Finn's question caught Pete off guard and he frowned. "Not that I know of."

"Do you know where Malina's keys are?" Finn wasn't going to let it drop. A safe-deposit box was the only other place he could imagine where Malina might have put a package.

"Uh, I don't know, maybe in her purse?"

"I'll get it," Eva offered, getting up from the table.

Finn was glad to have a few minutes alone with Pete. "You're telling me that you didn't once suspect your wife was using drugs?"

"Yes. That's exactly what I'm telling you. Why would I suspect Malina of doing something like that?" Anger flashed in Pete's dark eyes. "Sure, it's easy to look back now and see the signs, but at the time, I thought she was struggling with losing her eyesight. Her vision had got dramatically worse in those last few months before…" His voice trailed off.

"Before she was killed," Finn finished. "I've officially requested to reopen the investigation on her death. I'm not convinced it was an accident."

The blood drained from Pete's face and Finn knew he was truly shocked. "You—you think she was murdered?"

Finn wasn't sure how much to tell him. "I think it was meant to be a warning—return the package or else. Only they didn't realize how bad her vision was. She didn't react in time to jump out of the way and was killed rather than getting a little banged up."

Pete dropped his head into his hands, his body slumped as if he didn't possess an ounce of energy. Finn actually found himself feeling bad for the man.

"It's all so surreal. Finding out that Malina was using drugs and was killed over some stupid package that she stole." Pete lifted his head, his expression full of angst. "She had abdominal surgery five months ago, her appendix burst so they had to open her up. It's possible that's when she got hooked on painkillers, but to steal from her suppliers? Why on earth would she do that? Why?"

Finn remained silent, unable to provide an answer to Pete's questions. The guy appeared sincerely distraught and, as much as he'd hoped to get key information, Finn sensed he was wasting his time.

Pete hadn't known anything about what he suspected was Malina's apparent drug use or her activities. As sad as it was, the spouse was sometimes the last to know.

Eva returned to the kitchen carrying the purse she'd discovered during their earlier search. "Found the keys." She tossed the key ring on the table.

Finn picked it up before Pete could to examine each of the three keys. "Which one is the house key?"

"This one." Eva pointed at the dark brass key. "And this one is to the back door."

"And the third?" Finn held that one up.

Eva frowned. "That looks like it might be for the guide dog training center. I'll get my keys so we can compare."

The training center? Finn found it curious that Malina would have a key after being fired. Wouldn't Wade have asked for it back?

Eva returned and offered her key in comparison. They were a match. Finn nodded and took the keys. "I'll need to borrow these for a little while, then I'll get them back to you."

"Whatever."

Eva snapped her fingers. "Oh, by the way, you should know I found this cash, too." She set the five crisp one-hundred-dollar bills on the table in front of her brother-in-law.

"Five hundred dollars?" Pete stared at the cash as if it were a snake that would lash out and bite him. "Drug money?"

Finn exchanged a knowing glance with Eva. That was exactly what they'd thought, but there was no reason to add to Pete's distress. "We don't know that it's drug money. It could be from something else."

"Yeah? Like what?" Pete roughly pushed the bills toward Finn. "Take it away. I don't want it." He stood abruptly and moved to the other side of the room. "I'm finished answering your questions. I need some time alone."

"Pete, please..." Eva reached out to touch his arm, but he moved away.

"Not now, Eva. I need some peace and quiet. Time alone with Mikey. I have the next few days off work, and I'd like to spend that time with my son."

"I understand." Finn rose to his feet. "But you need to remember to stay inside for the next few days. I'll keep a squad posted outside your home, but until we get the guy who dognapped Cocoa, you and Mikey are still in danger. And so is Eva. I'd like her to stay here tonight."

Pete looked through the window at the police car that was parked in his driveway. "Yeah, that's fine."

"I can head home," Eva interjected. "I think Pete and Mikey have been through enough. They deserve time alone."

"I don't like that idea," Finn protested. "If you insist on leaving, then you need to stay in a hotel."

"I'll figure something out."

Finn wasn't sure he trusted that she'd actually go to the hotel, although he did see that she had her own suitcase packed and ready to go. "I'll drive you."

She looked as if she wanted to argue, but he held up the keys. "We'll make a stop at the training center first, if you don't mind."

She looked relieved and nodded. "Sure."

Pete turned from the window. "There's no reason to leave, Eva. I didn't intend to make you feel unwelcome. The sofa is yours for as long as you want it."

"Thanks, Pete, but I think you and Mikey deserve some quality father-son time. He's missed you." She gave Pete's arm a gentle squeeze, then retrieved her purse and looked at Finn expectantly. "Ready?"

Finn nodded and picked up Abernathy's food and water dishes, along with her duffel bag.

As they headed outside to his SUV, he hoped taking Eva with him to search the guide dog training center wasn't a mistake.

FOURTEEN

The training center looked different at night with only one light shining through the front window. It was well after eleven o'clock, so Eva knew none of the caretakers for the puppies would be around. As Finn parked his SUV and got out, she followed suit, feeling nervous for some reason, as if they were doing something wrong. They weren't, since Finn had taken a good hour to jump through the hoops to obtain a warrant, but still it felt deceitful for some reason.

Finn let Abernathy out of the back, and together the three of them approached the front entrance.

Malina's key, which looked shiny and new compared to hers, unlocked the front door. Since finding Malina's key, she'd tried to understand why her sister would have made a copy for herself. Why would Malina have needed access to the training center after being let go? Eva had no clue. Using this place as a hiding spot for the package was risky. There were plenty of people who went in and out of the training center. Too many to make sure you could get in and out without being noticed.

Unless of course Malina had done exactly what they were doing. Going inside at night.

As they entered, the puppies in the back kennel began to bark. She wanted to go there to reassure them but followed Finn and Abernathy into the office area.

"We're searching for the missing package," he told her. "Nothing more."

She nodded. "I can look through the drawers in the reception area."

"Thanks."

Leaving Finn to look through Wade's office, something she'd rather not do anyway, Eva went through the small reception area. There weren't many hiding places in general, and she found nothing in any of the drawers located along the right-hand side of the desk.

The dogs' barking was getting on her nerves, so after verifying there was no sign of the mysterious package, she went back to the kennel area.

"It's okay," she crooned. "It's just me."

The dogs continued to bark, wanting out of their kennels. She didn't blame them. Seeing them like this was always difficult for her. The puppies stayed alone in the kennels during their basic training, starting when they are eight weeks old, until they were twelve weeks old. Once that was finished, they went with trainers to be fostered for almost a year before returning to the center for formal training. Still, it wasn't easy to turn her back on them.

"Find anything?" she asked, returning to the office area.

"Just another bit of white powder." Finn held up an evidence bag. Eva squinted at it and saw a few grains of what might be cocaine.

"No package?"

"Nope." Finn tucked the evidence bag into his pocket, his expression reflected his frustration. "There must be somewhere else to search. Why else would Malina have a key?"

"There's a storeroom in the back near the kennels," she offered. "It's mostly filled with dog food and treats, along with some spare supplies."

Finn's green eyes brightened with excitement. "Show me."

She led the way back toward the kennels and opened the supply closet. They never kept it locked since it didn't house anything of real value, unless you counted the dog food.

Thinking of that made her worry about Cocoa. Did the stinky guy still have the puppy? Was he taking care of the animal? Feeding him regularly? Was stinky guy aware that puppies needed to be fed twice a day? It was horrible to think that Cocoa might be suffering at the hands of the man who would clearly do anything to get his stolen package back.

She prayed that Cocoa wasn't being mistreated and would be returned safe and sound.

Soon.

There wasn't a lot of space in the closet for two people and a K-9 partner, so she stayed back and let Finn perform the search. Abernathy was excited about the supply closet, no doubt smelling the food and treats within. Starting at the top, Finn moved everything around on the shelves, looked into a large box of doggy treats and made his way to the bottom shelves. There was a giant bag of dog food in the corner and she saw him eyeing it speculatively.

"You're not planning to dump all the food out, are you?"

"Yeah, I am." He hauled the bag toward him, shooing Abernathy out of the way. "The bottom of a bag of dog food would be a great hiding place."

"Until the bag is empty," she argued. Glancing around, she looked for something to use. "You can't just toss the food on the floor."

"Give me a minute to feel around in there." He shoved his hand into the bag, wiggling it all the way down until his entire arm was encased in brown pellets. A few were knocked onto the floor and quickly gobbled up by Abernathy.

Despite the seriousness of the situation, her

lips curved into a smile. Finn looked ridiculous, and she didn't for one minute believe that Malina had buried the stolen package in the bottom of a bag of dog food.

"Can you find something I can use to empty part of the bag?" He glanced over his shoulder, frowning when he noticed her grin. "What's so funny?"

"You. This." She waved a hand. "Give it up, Finn. We don't have anything to put all this food in. If we did, we wouldn't keep it in the bag. Besides, you're not thinking logically. How would Malina get the package to the bottom of the bag in the first place? Look at how you're struggling, and you're much stronger than my sister would have been."

He didn't give up for several long minutes. When he finally pulled his arm out from the bag, it was covered in brown crumbs. He tried to brush them off, but without much success, especially since Abernathy eagerly licked them up before he could stop him.

"Sit," Finn commanded.

Abernathy sat, which didn't prevent him from taking another few licks.

Eva giggled. "You look ridiculous. There's a bathroom over there." She gestured to the staff restroom.

"Stay," Finn ordered.

The yellow Lab's large brown eyes looked

mournful as Finn crossed over to the bathroom. Eva knew she shouldn't, but she wanted to give Abernathy a treat to reward him for being a good boy.

Instead, she reached down to scratch the silky spot between his ears.

When Finn returned he pulled a small doggy treat out of his pocket. Abernathy went still, his gaze locked on Finn. Finn gave him several commands, all of which Abernathy executed perfectly, before rewarding the K-9 with the treat.

"I like to use toys when training, but figured he was pretty well behaved surrounded by food like that." Finn shrugged. "He's a good partner."

"You make a good team." She pushed the bag of dog food back into the corner and closed the door. "I guess that's it, then."

"Yeah." Finn looked disappointed.

"It bothers me that you found cocaine in the office," she said as they made their way back through the center to the front door. "Malina hasn't been here for at least four months, and we have a cleaning crew that comes in once a week."

"Maybe they're not a very good cleaning crew." Finn relocked the front door and headed toward the SUV. "Clearly, your boss is overpaying for their services."

"Maybe." She'd never noticed the lack of cleaning before now. And since the white powder was in the office, where Malina had often sat to do the books, she thought it was odd that Wade Yost hadn't noticed the mess. Normally her boss didn't tolerate mediocrity.

It was likely he'd been distracted with the center being broken into and Cocoa being dog-napped. A thorough cleaning job wasn't high on his list of priorities.

"Which hotel?" Finn asked once they were seated in the SUV.

She wrinkled her nose. "I'd rather just go back to my place. I'm sure it's safe enough. No one would expect to find me there tonight. And by tomorrow, you'll have the stinky guy in custody."

"Eva." Finn let out an exasperated sigh. "We already discussed this. I'd feel better if you stayed in a hotel."

She pursed her lips, then turned in her seat to face him. "Finn, with my vision issues it's hard for me to be in a strange place, especially at night. I'd really rather be surrounded by my own things in a room where I know exactly where the furniture is located."

He drew his hand over his face in a resigned gesture. "Okay, fine. I'll drive you to your place."

She narrowed her gaze, distrustful of how easily he'd capitulated. But he didn't say anything more, simply turning right and taking the familiar route to the small house she shared with her two college roommates.

Finn carried in her duffel bag, then insisted

on searching through the house with Abernathy to make sure no one was hiding inside. She unpacked her things, noticing that one of her roommates had swept up the broken glass on the floor of her bedroom.

"I could sleep on your sofa," Finn offered when she joined him in the living room.

"I don't think that's a good idea. I'm not entirely sure whether or not Alecia or Julie are working tonight. I think they're still staying at the hotel, but if for some reason they come home unexpectedly, they'll be shocked to see you."

Finn didn't look happy as he shrugged. "Okay, that's fine. Sleep well, Eva. Come, Abernathy."

The yellow Lab trotted over to Finn's side. Eva walked them to the door and stood in the doorway, watching as they headed toward Finn's car.

"Bye," she said before shutting the door and locking it. She walked back into the living room, feeling vulnerable and alone.

She pulled out her phone to call Finn, ready to ask him to come back and sleep on the sofa. She stopped herself and slipped the device back into her pocket.

Leaning on Finn the way she had over the past few days had to stop. She needed to be independent. Finn had watched the rearview mirror like a hawk, so there was no way they could have been followed. No one knew she was home.

Staying here was perfectly safe.

And maybe if she told herself that over and over again, she'd be able to shake off the sense of unease long enough to believe it.

Finn drove his SUV around the block, looking for a sign of someone who might be watching Eva's place. He didn't see anything out of the ordinary, and no one resembling the sketch she'd made of the stinky guy.

No matter how safe Eva likely was there, he couldn't bring himself to leave. If anything happened to her, he'd never forgive himself.

He made a second loop around the block before pulling into the driveway and parking his vehicle in front of the two-story house. The light was still on in Eva's room, but the rest of the place was dark. He waited, wondering if she'd look out to find him sitting there, half expecting her to come out to confront him, but she didn't.

After cracking the windows open on either side to let the fresh air circulate through the interior of the SUV, he put his seat as far back as it could go and tried to relax.

Sitting in the car wasn't remotely comfortable because he couldn't stretch his long legs all the way out, but he'd been in worse situations, so he made the best of it. He yawned and shifted in his seat. With the windows open, he should hear the sounds of traffic going by and, hopefully, would also hear if anyone tried to approach the place.

Thankfully, Abernathy's keen hearing would alert Finn to anything he might miss.

He stared at the house wondering how he'd ended up here. Somehow, he'd instinctively known she'd pull something like this. Eva was stubborn, especially when it came to maintaining her independence, and while he admired that about her, at times like this he found it frustrating.

"Women," he said to Abernathy. "Sure, I like to have fun. Normally it takes only two dates for me to know it's time to move on. Yet here we are. I'm telling you, I have no clue why I'm letting this woman get under my skin."

Abernathy yawned and then, as if in agreement, shook his head, making his ears flap.

Finn thought about their fruitless search of the guide dog training center. He'd thought for sure that he'd find the package hidden in there somewhere. Why else would Malina have kept a key to the place?

The shiny brand-new key nagged at him. Obviously, Malina had got it made just prior to being let go. Had she known Wade Yost was onto her drug use? She must have suspected the hammer was coming down or she wouldn't have had time to get the key made. He had to believe Yost would have taken the key from her after firing her. And again, why had she bothered? Was it possible she'd had the package hidden in the training center for a short time? Maybe as a temporary hiding place? It clearly wasn't there now.

Unless Wade Yost had found it. As soon as the thought popped into his head, Finn disregarded it. Yost would have notified the authorities about something like that.

Eva might be right in concluding that Malina had used the drugs or spent the money that they were relentlessly searching for. Their best chance of cracking this case open was to convince Roach to talk in exchange for a lighter sentence.

Coming across the small dusting of white powder had been interesting. He'd have it matched to the other samples they'd found, but he wasn't sure that information would add much to the investigation. Malina was the common denominator between three of the four locations where they'd recovered the drugs. The house she shared with Pete, the locker at The Fitness Club and now the training center. Matching them to the drugs they'd found in the apartment Roach was using would connect the drug dealer to Malina, which wasn't necessarily a surprise, either. Not if Malina had stolen the package from them.

Roach was small-time. No way was he in charge of the entire operation. Zach mentioned something about the kingpin being known as Uno, whatever that stood for.

Finn turned his thoughts back to Grant Ulrich, the owner of The Fitness Club and the furniture store across from the LaGuardia airport. That was a key connection and he made a mental note to talk to the DA tomorrow about his requirements related to Roach's deal. Finding Cocoa was a top priority, but so was obtaining the name and identity of the leader in charge of the drug ring.

So far, the bit of background he'd dug up on Ulrich hadn't provided any clues that might be used against him. No sudden influx of cash or outgoing cash or any other red flags in his bank account. But he hadn't been able to get into the books related to the two businesses. Finn planned to dig deeper into The Fitness Club and the furniture store first thing in the morning. After he dropped off the latest bit of evidence he'd found at the training center.

The window of Eva's bedroom went dark. Finn glanced at his watch and realized it was nearing midnight. He decided to take Abernathy out one last time. The K-9 sniffed around Eva's house for what seemed like an eternity before doing his business. Back inside the SUV, Finn relaxed against his reclined seat, ready to settle in for the night.

Sleep didn't come easy. He could blame it on the fact that sleeping in a car was never restful, but the real reason was that his mind was overwhelmed with thoughts of Eva.

Pete had interrupted their kiss and Finn wished he'd kissed her earlier. Okay, sure, logically he shouldn't have kissed her at all, but his common sense had apparently taken a long hike up a steep mountain.

Tomorrow. He'd get back on track tomorrow. Breaking Roach was key. Once they had the stinky guy in custody and Cocoa back with Eva where he belonged, life would get back to normal.

It occurred to him that after spending these past four days with Eva, he wasn't so sure what normal would feel like. Letting her go wasn't going to be as easy as it had been to move on from the other women he'd dated.

In fact, he and Eva hadn't even gone out on a date. Unless you counted dinner at Griffin's, which had ended abruptly with Mikey's kidnapping.

He'd told her not to underestimate him with regard to her diagnosis, but that wasn't what would ultimately keep them apart. Despite the fact that Luke Hathaway and Zach Jameson had both recently got engaged, he was convinced that marrying a cop was a proven path to unhappiness. A relationship like that wasn't for him.

Imagining a future without Eva caused his heart to ache for what he'd never have, so he did his best to push those thoughts aside. Instead, he concentrated on watching the cars going by on the street in front of Eva's house.

Despite his efforts to stay alert, Finn must

have dozed off, because Abernathy's whine woke him up.

"Huh?" He rubbed the grit from his eyes and glanced back at his K-9 partner. "What is it, boy?"

Abernathy had his nose pressed up against the side window of the SUV. A chill snaked down Finn's spine, and he peered through the darkness trying to figure out what had caught Abernathy's attention.

Yellow Labs normally weren't as protective as German shepherds, but remembering how Abernathy had latched onto Roach's leg, preventing him from escaping the window, made Finn take the dog's whining seriously.

He couldn't see anything suspicious. There was no sign of movement from anywhere near the house from what he could tell. Was it possible that Abernathy had seen a chipmunk or squirrel?

Unwilling to ignore his partner's alert, he pushed open the driver's-side door and went around to the back, intending to let Abernathy out.

The dog gave several sharp barks. Finn instinctively turned, lifting his arm to protect his head, but a second too late. Something hard slammed into his temple. Pain reverberated through his neck and skull, and then there was only darkness.

FIFTEEN

A muffled thud woke Eva from a restless slumber. She lay in her bed for several long seconds, straining to listen. Just when she thought the noise had been nothing more than a neighbor coming home late, she heard it again, louder.

She sat upright in bed, her gaze raking through the darkness of her room.

Someone was inside the house!

For a moment she considered the possibility that one of her roommates had decided to come home after a late shift at the hospital, having got fed up with staying at the hotel. Still, she sensed something was wrong. Sliding silently from her bed, she thought about what she might use as a weapon. Grabbing the ceramic lamp off her bedside table, she pulled the cord from the socket, then plastered herself against the wall, holding it ready. If the noise was from her roommates, they wouldn't bother coming to her room.

She held her breath and waited. There was no

point in trying to see through the darkness. Her eyes wouldn't help her now. Instead, she focused on the room layout that was etched in her memory.

Should she try to get out through the one window that wasn't boarded up? It was a long drop to the ground, but it might be worth breaking a leg or worse in order to escape from the intruder.

Heart pounding with fear, she decided there wasn't enough time to get out through the window. Inching along the wall toward the doorway of her bedroom, she mentally prepared herself for the worst. Where was Finn? She never should have refused his offer to sleep on the sofa. Her heightened senses made it easy to track the sound of the intruder moving up the stairs to the second floor.

Maybe she should have grabbed her phone instead, but it was too late now.

Dear Lord, help me! Keep me safe in Your care!

The scent of sweat made her wrinkle her nose. She lifted the lamp over her head. When she thought the stinky guy was in the doorway, she brought the lamp down hard against him.

Stinky made a grunting noise, but her aim must have been off, because he didn't go down. The lamp did, though, crashing against the hardwood floor and breaking into pieces. She heard him fumbling in the darkness and made a break for it.

She darted for the opposite side of the room to the window that wasn't boarded up. As she yanked the sash upward, the stinky guy grabbed her roughly from behind, turning and shoving her hard up against the wall.

"No! Let me go!" She screamed and struggled against him, kicking and punching, hoping and praying someone might hear the scuffle. If not her roommates, who were still at the hotel, then maybe a neighbor? Someone out with their dog? Anyone?

Stinky leaned his forearm against her throat, pressing hard. She grabbed at it with both hands, desperate to free herself, realizing in some dim recess of her mind that it was the same arm she'd scratched with her keys the day he stole Cocoa. It was no use. His strength was enough to silence her screams, making her gasp for air.

"Where's the package?" The hint of Southern twang in his tone was more pronounced with his anger.

Eva tried to answer, but nothing emerged from her throat other than a croak. She could feel herself growing dizzy and knew if he didn't move his arm she'd black out.

The stinky guy must have realized she couldn't breathe and eased back some of the pressure. She drew in a deep ragged breath, sucking in desperately needed oxygen into her lungs.

"I don't know where my sister hid the package," she finally managed. "I looked through the entire house twice without finding anything other than five hundred dollars. Is that what you're looking for? Money?"

"Five hundred is nothing," he sneered. "The drug package your sister stole from us is worth over fifty grand."

Fifty thousand dollars? Oh, Malina, what did you do? What were you thinking?

"Why did my sister have the package in the first place?" she asked.

"You didn't know that your sweet sister was one of our best drug couriers?"

Drug courier? Malina? No! When? How? Her silent questions tumbled through her mind like a kaleidoscope, creating a new picture at every turn.

His tone grew sinister. "Until she double-crossed us. We sent her a message, sideswiping her with the truck. Killing her wasn't part of the plan. We'd wanted to get the package back before eliminating her for good."

Nausea churned in her gut as she realized Malina's death was a direct result of stealing drugs. No doubt, these stupid men had no idea that her sister was going blind and wouldn't have seen the truck swerving toward her until it was too late. Her sister's death wasn't an accident—it was murder.

Swallowing hard, Eva focused on how to keep

him talking. Finding a way to get him out of the house was her best opportunity to escape.

"I have a key to the training center," she offered. "I'll help you search for the package. I know every nook and cranny in the place."

He was silent for a moment as if considering her offer. Then he slapped her across the face. The unanticipated blow shocked her. Sharp pain radiated through her jaw, and tears sprang to her eyes.

"Don't lie to me," he spit. "I followed you and that cop boyfriend of yours from the training center. I know you already searched the place."

He followed them? And knew about Finn? Eva's hopes of escaping and being rescued plummeted to the soles of her feet.

Before she could gather herself to ask more questions, he removed his arm and yanked her from the wall. He turned and held her shoulders in a steely grip while pushing her out of her room and into the hallway.

Her attempts to fight against him were like swatting harmlessly at a pesky fly. He fended off her flailing hands easily and wrapped his strong arms around her chest, squeezing hard. Half dragging, half carrying, he took her down to the main level and shoved her onto a kitchen chair. A chair that he must have dragged into the living room, as she could see a hint of light streaming in through the window facing the street.

He'd obviously planned this from the very beginning. Why he'd brought her down here, she couldn't be sure, other than she didn't have any furniture in her room. Less objects for her to bump into, the better.

"What are you doing?" Her voice was hoarse with fear.

His dark shape towered over her. She couldn't help shrinking away from him, anticipating another physical assault.

"Silencing you for good. The police have got too close and our boss is worried Roach is going to turn us in. It's time to get out of Dodge."

Eva tried not to react to his statement but was afraid the truth was reflected on her face. She heard a ripping noise and felt something sticky against her wrist. When she realized he was using duct tape to secure her, she fought him off with every last ounce of strength she possessed.

He used his knee to keep her pinned in the chair, leaning all his weight on her as he finished securing her other wrist. Then he did the same with her feet. "Too bad you never found the package. You could have avoided all of this."

Rendered completely helpless by his binds, she could only watch as he bent over to pull some sort of backpack off the floor. More proof that he'd come prepared. He'd brought his bag of tricks, including the duct tape, to finish her off once and for all.

"This will never work." She tried to infuse confidence into her wobbly voice. "Finn will hunt you down, no matter where you run. And killing me won't prevent Roach from turning evidence against you and your boss."

"Finn? Is that his name?" Stinky surprised her by dropping something furry in her lap. The puppy let out little yips of fear, squirming against her. Cocoa! She hoped the puppy would remember her scent and be reassured by her presence. "Don't worry, I've already taken care of him. And Roach won't live to see another day to implicate us, either. We can get to him even while he's in jail. You should know anything is possible for the right price." After uttering that last statement, he slapped a four-inch length of tape over her mouth, silencing her.

No! Finn! Her heart squeezed as horror washed over her. Was it possible the stinky guy would find a way to kill everyone who knew what they were up to? All because of a package of drugs worth fifty grand?

Cocoa buried his face against her stomach and she wished she could cuddle him close.

Stinky disappeared from view. She thought maybe he'd finally left her alone in the house, and then the acrid scent of gasoline hit hard.

In that moment she knew that he intended to burn down the entire house with her and Cocoa trapped inside.

Smoke wafted toward her. Had he started by putting the living room furniture on fire? Using her shoulder, she rubbed at the edge of the tape covering her mouth. It took several attempts before she could feel it coming loose. She bent her face to her hands and used her fingers to pull it the rest of the way off.

"Help! Please, help!" Fearing no one was close enough to hear her screams, she bent over and used her teeth in an attempt to get the binds loose. Cocoa pushed his nose between her face and her wrist, getting in the way. She didn't want to hurt the puppy—he'd been through enough—so she tried to merely nudge him aside. But he persisted and helped her by using his small sharp teeth to assist in ripping the tape from around her wrist.

Even with Cocoa's help, it was an arduous task, taking far longer than she'd anticipated. Smoke filled the room, burning her eyes and likely Cocoa's, too. They were watering so badly she had to close them while continuing to work at the binding holding her right wrist hostage against the arm of the chair.

After what seemed like forever, the tape gave way. Using her right hand and her teeth, she managed to free her left hand and then her feet. Now the living room was filled with smoke, rendering her completely blind.

A wave of panic hit hard, and she knew that this was exactly what she'd be like in a couple of years. Completely blind. Unable to find her way around without help.

If she lived that long.

Cuddling Cocoa to her chest with one hand, she crawled along the floor toward the door. The increasing sense of heat against her face gave her pause. She needed to get away from the fire, not move closer to it.

Stinky had set the fire near the doorway, effectively blocking her escape route. She turned and crawled toward the wall containing the large picture window. Heat radiated from that way, too.

Which way should she go? Eva cowered on the floor with Cocoa, fear rising in her throat like a wave of bile. The pup lurched forward, but Eva hung back, fearing it was useless.

They were trapped!

The sound of Abernathy's frenzied barking penetrated the darkness in his mind. It took Finn a moment to realize he was lying on the driveway behind his SUV. With a low groan, he placed a hand on the rear bumper and used that to lever himself upright. His stomach gave a sickening lurch, the pounding in his head matching the beat of his heart. He felt the lump on his temple, his fingers detecting the stickiness of blood. Willing himself to ignore the pain, he opened the back hatch, allowing Abernathy to jump down.

His K-9 partner was beside himself, weaving

around his legs, tail wagging as he sniffed at his hands and clothes. As much as he wanted to give his partner some well-deserved reassurance, there wasn't a moment to waste.

"Come, Abernathy." He looked toward the home Eva shared with her roommates, assuming the guy who'd hit him had gone inside to find her. Seeing the flicker of yellow through the window sent his heart up into his throat.

The house was on fire!

Eva!

He lifted his hand to his radio to call it in just as a man darted from the house. Finn barked into the radio as he moved. "This is unit twelve, I need backup and fire trucks to fight a fire!" He rattled off Eva's address. "Get him," he said to Abernathy, using a hand signal to send his K-9 partner after the perp.

Abernathy took off, following the guy down the street.

Finn hated the idea of sending his partner off alone, but he couldn't leave Eva inside the burning house.

He rushed up to the front door and yanked it open, grateful to find that the perp hadn't bothered to lock it on his way out. The kitchen curtains were in flames, and he feared the worst. That he was too late. He took two steps, then tripped over something soft.

"Umph." The muffled sound was followed by several hacking coughs.

"Eva?" Somehow, he'd managed to avoid falling directly on top of her. Relieved she was still alive, yet concerned she wasn't able to talk, Finn scrambled to his feet. He reached down for her, trying to peer through the smoky air. "Are you okay?"

Still coughing from the smoke, she didn't answer, Finn put his arm beneath her shoulders and helped her upright. He was about to swing her into his arms, when he heard a high-pitched bark. Cocoa? It had to be.

The perp had left her and Cocoa in the burning house to die.

"Keep holding on to the pup. I'll get you out of here." He lifted her up, cradling her in his arms as he took her outside into the fresh air. Carrying her to his SUV, he gently set her on her feet, then opened the passenger-side door, so she could sit down. With help from the streetlamp, he could see she still cradled Cocoa close to her chest.

"Are you hurt? Did you get burned by the fire?" He didn't like the sound of her cough and wondered how long she'd been trapped inside while he was lying unconscious on the pavement.

"No." Her voice was little more than a croak followed by several deep, hacking coughs. "Cocoa—helped show me—the way outside. I didn't—want to follow at first, but he showed me the way!"

"I'm so glad you're okay." The wail of sirens grew louder, filling the air as the police and fire trucks arrived, and he knew that help would be there soon. Now that Eva was safe, he needed to find his K-9 partner. "Stay here, Eva. I'll be back as soon as possible."

"Where—" A coughing fit interrupted whatever she was about to say.

"Abernathy is tracking the perp. I'll be back soon." This time he didn't hesitate, taking off in the direction he'd sent his K-9 partner.

Following the sounds of Abernathy's barking was harder than he'd thought. The sound echoed off the buildings, making it difficult to pinpoint his partner's exact location. He hadn't been in the smoky house for long, but he still found it difficult to see through the darkness and realized this was what Eva faced each day.

Still, he pushed on, ignoring the pounding in his head. He went several blocks and came upon a dead-end alley where he found Abernathy barking his head off. The perp was trying to squeeze through a narrow opening between a fence and a brick building.

"Stop! Police!" Finn's voice cut through Abernathy's barking.

The man turned and in that moment Finn realized he had a gun. But instead of pointing the gun at Finn, the perp took aim at his K-9 partner.

"Drop your weapon or I'll kill the dog."

There was a Southern twang in the guy's voice. Realizing he'd found the perp who'd stolen Cocoa, his mind raced. Would he shoot Abernathy? If that was his intent, he could have killed the dog before Finn had even arrived. And he hadn't killed Cocoa, either.

Then again, the stinky guy had left both Eva and Cocoa to die in a fire.

"I said drop your weapon!" Stinky shouted.

Training told him not to give up his weapon, but Finn couldn't risk losing Abernathy.

"Okay, okay." He lifted up both his hands, his gun pointing toward the sky in a gesture of surrender. "There's no reason to shoot the dog. I'm giving up my weapon, see?"

"Drop it. Now!"

Finn hesitated for a moment, then carefully bent over to set the gun on the ground.

"Kick it toward me."

Finn didn't move. The wailing sirens grew louder, and he noticed the perp glance jerkily toward the street as if searching for the red lights.

In that second, Finn jumped into action. "Get help!" He tossed the command toward Abernathy as he launched himself toward the stinky guy, hitting his gun arm hard in an effort to knock the gun loose.

The stinky guy was stronger than Finn had given him credit for. Despite holding the guy's wrist tightly, squeezing as hard as he could to force him to drop the weapon, the perp hung on, using his bulky frame in an attempt to knock Finn off balance. He nearly succeeded.

For several long moments they struggled to gain control of the weapon.

Boom!

The sound of gunfire echoed loudly around them, giving him one last chance to rip the weapon from the stinky guy's hand.

"Get down! Now!" Finn pressed the gun against the man's temple and he slowly went down to his knees, then stretched out until he was lying facedown on the ground.

Ripping his cuffs off his belt, he grabbed the stinky guy's wrists and locked them together. Once he had the perp secure, he lifted his gaze and swept the area, searching for Abernathy.

He'd hoped his K-9 had gone to get backup, but that wasn't the case. His K-9 partner came toward him, limping as he favored his right back leg.

"What happened, boy?" he asked.

Abernathy was wearing his vest, but as he came closer, Finn could see blood dripping from the animal's flank.

His partner was wounded!

SIXTEEN

The oxygen mask over her face eased her spasmodic coughing but made talking difficult. "Where's Finn?" she asked in a muffled and hoarse voice. She'd asked several times already without a response.

"Just take it easy." One of the paramedics leaned over to check the monitor she was connected to. "You're doing great. The oxygen levels in your blood are close to normal."

Keeping one arm around Cocoa, who was content to cuddle close, she used the other hand to move the mask to the side. "I'll be better when you get one of the officers over here to talk to me. I need to know where Officer Gallagher is and that he's safe."

The paramedic replaced the oxygen mask over her face. "Someone will be here soon," he reassured her.

She didn't want *someone*. She wanted *Finn*.

She needed to know he was okay and that someone had gone after him to provide backup.

A loud popping noise had her jerking the mask
off her face again. "Was that a gunshot?"

Instant chaos ensued, confirming her suspi-
cion. Dozens of officers and firefighters swarmed
the area, apparently searching for the source of
the gunshot. Through it all, firefighters continued spraying their hoses at Alecia's house in an
effort to douse the flames. Two more hoses were
aimed at the houses on each side to protect them
from damage. She was horrified about Alecia's
house and was thankful her friend's parents had
insisted on them paying for good insurance.

The paramedic replaced her oxygen mask,
staying close to her side. She appreciated his
gesture of support and was secretly glad Pete
was home with Mikey instead of being out here,
fighting the fire. While she was no expert, the
fire appeared to be under control. Maybe because
the source of the blaze had been focused in the
living room.

Remembering those terrifying moments when
she'd feared she was trapped inside the house
made her shudder. Cocoa had wiggled out of her
arms and had let out several barks while headed
toward the doorway leading to the kitchen. She'd
followed the puppy, shying away from the heat
on her left and keeping far to the right. When
the heat was behind them and the floor changed

from hardwood to tile, she knew they'd made it. The front door wasn't far. She had scooped Cocoa close and continued crawling toward the door leading outside.

She'd been grateful Finn had literally stumbled upon her in the doorway and that he was all right. His familiar musky scent had calmed her racing heart, but then he'd left her to go after the stinky guy.

Lord, please keep Finn and Abernathy safe in Your care!

Praying was second nature now, and she knew she had Finn to thank for bringing her back to her faith. He was the one who'd shown her the power of prayer. He was the only man who'd kissed her while knowing her diagnosis.

It was impossible to imagine life without him.

She secretly acknowledged that her feelings for Finn went beyond friendship. But knowing that didn't change her future blindness. With her eyes still burning and tearing up from the smoke, she couldn't see clearly. Being faced with the reality of her future was sobering. Looking back on what had transpired with Malina, she understood that her surgery, along with facing blindness, was the catalyst for her sister's desperate foray into crime.

Nothing else made sense.

"Eva?" It wasn't Finn's voice, yet it was familiar. She squinted through the group of people still milling about to find her boss, Wade Yost, making his way toward her. "You found Cocoa!"

She hadn't exactly found the puppy—the stinky guy had tossed him at her—but nodded anyway. "Yes, thankfully. What are you doing here?"

"I heard about the fire on the news and rushed over." Her boss elbowed the paramedic out of the way, dropping to one knee beside her. The paramedic took a few steps away as if to provide them some privacy. Wade reached out to lightly stroke Cocoa. "I'm so glad you're both okay."

It was odd that he'd come here in the middle of the night. And how had he known this was where she lived in the first place? Her address was on file at the training center, but it was a little creepy that he'd recognized the house from the news. Yet she told herself to get over it. He hadn't revealed the truth about Malina because he hadn't wanted to lose Eva as a trainer. She appreciated his support. "Me, too. Cocoa helped me get out through the fire. He's going to make an awesome guide dog."

"I believe you." Wade smiled, and then she felt something blunt and hard poke into her side. "Now, listen to me. We're going to walk away from here, understand? You make one false move and I'll shoot you right here. With all the chaos, they'll never catch me, and you'll be dead from the blood loss before anyone can help."

A gun? She froze, her mind scrambling to understand what was happening. Wade was her boss. He ran the guide dog training center. Why was he doing this?

"Take that oxygen mask off and stand up. We're going to take a little walk."

After removing the face mask, she rose from her seat at the edge of the ambulance bumper. Casting a furtive glance toward the paramedic, she hoped and prayed he'd notice something was amiss. But he was in deep conversation with another firefighter. She took two steps, then stopped. "I'm still connected to the monitor."

Wade yanked the cords off her in a swift movement. Though the monitor alarm beeped, the sound was lost amid the chaos of people talking and rushing water, and no one seemed to notice. That simply reinforced what Wade had threatened. He could shoot her now and ditch the gun, and no one would be any wiser.

Feeling helpless once again, she walked alongside Wade, still cuddling with Cocoa. They crossed the street, leaving the paramedics and firefighters behind.

"Where are we going?" She did everything she could to drag her feet, unwilling to leave the relative safety of the police and firefighters behind.

"The training center. The big boss wants to meet you."

The big boss? The one in charge of the drug

running? Was this how her sister had been led astray? Why would Wade have fired Malina if she was secretly working for him? Did her termination have to do with stealing the package of drugs?

Eva sent one last desperate glance over her shoulder searching for someone, anyone who might help.

Nothing good would come from meeting the big boss. And she knew that this time, there was a good chance she wouldn't survive.

Finn kept his knee wedged in the center of the stinky guy's back as he gently probed Abernathy's wound. It didn't look too deep, thankfully, just a bit of a gash but he still needed to get his partner to the vet ASAP.

"You'll be okay, boy." He gave Abernathy a one-armed hug, then shifted his weight off the prone perp. "Get up." He grabbed the guy beneath his arm, helping him stagger to his feet.

"I'll cut a deal." The guy's twang had turned whiny. "I'll give you the big boss."

"What's your name?" Finn asked, pushing him toward the road. He could see cops milling around, but they hadn't stumbled upon the narrow alley.

Finn wasn't sure he would have found it, either, if not for Abernathy.

"Stu Greer," was the grudging response.

"Well, Stu, you're under arrest for arson and attempted murder of a police officer, among other crimes." He rattled off the Miranda warning, then added, "I'm not sure that a deal is in your future."

"I'll give you the big boss," Greer repeated. "And I didn't attempt to shoot your dog. The gun went off by accident."

"Yeah, yeah." Finn didn't doubt that Greer's lawyer would play that angle. "Come, Abernathy."

Gamely, his K-9 partner kept pace beside him, and Finn wished he could carry his partner to safety. When he reached the street, he waved a uniformed officer over. "Take this guy for me, would you? My partner is injured."

The officer nodded and took Greer's other arm. Finn bent down and lifted his seventy-five-pound yellow Lab into his arms. Abernathy licked him on the cheek.

He strode quickly toward the spot where he'd left Eva. The cop urged Greer along as well, keeping pace. He noticed the fire crew had doused the flames inside Eva's home, and they continued to pour water on the building to be safe. In the summer heat any spark they missed could easily ignite a second fire.

"Where's Eva Kendall?" He raked his gaze over the area. When he noticed the ambulance in the center of the street, with some sort of wires lying across the bumper, a bad feeling settled in his chest. "Eva? Eva!"

At the sound of his shout, the paramedic glanced over at him, then looked at the empty spot where the monitor was quietly alarming. "Hey, where did she go?"

Finn set Abernathy just inside the ambulance. "I need you to clean him up and put antibiotic ointment on his wound."

"I don't treat dogs," the paramedic protested.

"You do now." Finn wasn't about to take no for an answer. He raked his gaze over the crowd, searching in vain for Eva's blond hair. "How long as she been gone?"

"Just a minute or two." The paramedic was grudgingly using gauze to wipe away the blood from Abernathy's flank injury.

"Abernathy, stay." He gave the command before hurrying toward the street. It wasn't like Eva to wander off, especially since he'd told her he'd return. How well could she see anyway? Her eyes had been watering badly when he'd got her out of the house.

"Eva!" He raised his voice to be heard over the din. Several of the cops and firefighters glanced at him, but there was no sign of Eva.

He returned to the ambulance, where the uniformed officer was still holding Stu Greer. "Tell me about the big boss."

Stu sneered at him. "Not saying anything until I get my lawyer."

The words were similar to what Roach had said, only the guy still hadn't talked. Finn wanted to grab the cuffed man by the shoulders to shake him until his teeth rattled. But of course he couldn't. Instead, he stepped closer until he was invading Greer's personal space.

"If anything happens to Eva, I'll make sure you go down for her murder, understand? Now, tell me who the big boss is!"

Greer stared at him for a long moment before admitting, "We call him Uno. As in he's numero uno in the cartel."

"Number one?" That information wasn't the least bit helpful. He needed a name! "What else does *Uno* stand for? What's his real name?"

"Ulrich." Greer said the name so softly Finn almost didn't hear it. Then it clicked.

"Grant Ulrich? The owner of The Fitness Club and the furniture store?"

Greer nodded. "He owns a lot of places, uses them to launder drug money."

Finn remembered the white powder found in the office at the guide dog training center. "Does Ulrich own the guide dog training center? Is it part of the drug-running organization? Is that where he got the idea to use Cocoa as bait?"

"Yeah." Greer craned his neck to look back at the officer who still had him by the arm. "You're my witness. I gave him information to help his case, so I expect a lighter sentence, understand?"

Finn felt a chill snake down his spine at the implication of the training center. He glanced over at Abernathy lying in the back of the ambulance. The K-9 lifted his head, his dark eyes laser focused on Finn.

As much as he needed to get his partner to the vet, he sensed there wasn't a moment to waste. He crossed over to the ambulance. Cleaning the wound had helped and the gash didn't look deep enough to need stitches, yet he still wanted his partner to be checked out by the vet.

He debated between sending Abernathy to the vet without him or taking him along to find Eva. It wasn't an easy decision, but he needed his partner's keen scent. He lifted the dog and put him back on his feet.

"Come, Abernathy." Finn glanced around, then picked up the oxygen mask, hoping, praying there was enough of Eva's scent left behind for Abernathy to use. He held the face mask to Abernathy's nose. "Find. Find Eva."

Abernathy sniffed at the face mask, then went to work. He made a circle around the area in front of the ambulance, then trotted off in a direction that led across the street.

Finn followed, relieved that his partner was on Eva's trail. As they went down one bloc, then another, he saw the guide dog training center up ahead.

This time he wanted backup, so before they got too close he used his radio. "This is unit twelve, I need backup at the guide dog training center for a possible hostage situation."

There was static on the line, then another officer responded, "This is Zach Jameson. I'm on my way."

"Reed Branson and Jessie, also responding," another voice said.

"Ten-four." He continued toward the training center. Even from this distance, when they were still a few blocks away, he could see a dim light shining from the back of the building.

Interesting that it wasn't from the office area. He quickened his pace, then slowed down when he realized Abernathy was doing his best to keep up with him.

Abernathy alerted just outside the front door of the building. Finn praised him, then glanced over as Zach Jameson and his drug-sniffing beagle joined them. There was no sign of Reed, but Finn hoped he'd show up soon.

"I think Eva's in there with the big boss, a man named Grant Ulrich."

"The owner of The Fitness Club?" Zach's eyes widened.

"Yeah, he owns this place, too." Finn tried the handle and was surprised when it opened. He knew Eva had a key and wondered if she'd left the door open on purpose.

"I'll take the front. You and Eddie cover the back. Tell Branson to meet you there. His K-9, Jessie, will give us added strength." He glanced at his watch. "We'll breach the building in three minutes."

"Three minutes. Got it," Zach agreed. He and Eddie disappeared around the corner.

Finn eased into the building, moving as silently as possible. The sounds of dogs barking helped to cover the noise of Abernathy's pants. He felt terrible about delaying his partner's care, but was determined to get Eva out of here alive.

Above the barking din, he heard a man's deep gravelly voice. "Do you have any idea how much trouble you've caused me?"

"Me?" Eva's incredulous tone would have made him smile under different circumstances. But at the moment, he wanted her to play along rather than antagonize them.

"Where is the package?" The roar was a clear indication that Ulrich was losing his temper.

"I don't know!" Eva's hoarse yell was followed by a hacking cough. "Don't you think I would have given it to you by now if I had it? I couldn't care less about your stupid drugs!"

Finn flattened himself against the wall, edging closer. He held his weapon high near his ear, his attention focused on what he might find up ahead.

"Too bad. Without the package you are of no use to me. And I don't tolerate loose ends, which is why I had Wade fetch you for me. It's time to snip them off, one by one."

Finn's heart stuttered in his chest at the threat. What if he shot Eva before they were ready? The minutes were going by too slowly. Logically he knew he had to wait for Zach and hopefully Reed Branson to get in position, but standing there doing nothing was pure agony. He edged a little closer and risked a quick glance into the room.

Eva was standing between two men, one of them a stranger who was holding a gun on her. His gut twisted as he realized Wade Yost was there, too. Yost also held a gun, which meant he wasn't an innocent bystander. Yost had been involved all along. Finn knew the stranger holding Eva at gunpoint had to be Ulrich.

He rested back against the wall for a moment, committing the location of the principals to memory. With Eva standing between the two men, the likelihood of her being injured was far too high.

A diversion? He thought for a moment about sending a canister of tear gas inside, but he didn't have a mask and neither did Zach. The gas would hurt Eva and their K-9s' eyes, too.

No, they had to use their strength and instincts to take these two perps out, permanently if necessary. He stared at his watch, silently counting the seconds until it was go time.

Three, two, one. Now!

Finn heard the sound of Zach kicking open the back door as he stepped into the doorway. "Drop your weapons!" He waited a second, then yelled, "Eva, get down!" Yost lifted his weapon toward Eva, so he fired his gun at the same time another shot rang out.

Ulrich howled as he fell face forward, hitting the floor with a thud. Finn rushed in, getting to the prone figure of Yost before he could move. Both of their bullets had hit their marks. He stepped on the guy's wrist, pinning the gun to the floor as his gaze sought Eva.

She'd thrown herself down and to the left. Zach rushed over and held Ulrich down, disarming him.

"Eva? Are you okay?" Finn couldn't leave Yost until he had him secured, and since his cuffs were still on Greer, he'd have to use the plastic flex ties.

"Fine," she said in a weary voice followed by a muffled cough. "How did you find me?"

"Greer talked." He used the flex ties to secure Yost's wrists before dragging the man to his feet. "Did you hear that, Yost? Ulrich? Greer told us all about you in exchange for a deal on his sentencing."

Zach cuffed Ulrich's wrists behind him, then drew him up to his feet, too. "Well, look at that.

Eddie has caught the scent of drugs. What do you have hiding in your pockets?"

Abernathy had come over to sniff at Eva, licking her face as she rested on the floor as if she didn't possess the strength to get up.

When Zach began digging in Ulrich's pockets for whatever had caught Eddie's scent, the man lashed out with his booted foot toward Eddie and hit Abernathy instead. The toe of his boot connected hard with the injured spot on Abernathy's flank.

His partner yelped in pain as he went flying across the room beneath the force of the kick. His flank wound began to bleed, worse than before, and a red haze of fury filled Finn's vision.

"You just assaulted a police officer," he yelled.

Eva pushed herself upright, scooped Cocoa back into her arms and went to Abernathy. She glanced back at him, concern darkening her eyes. "Finn? We need to get him to the vet right away!"

Inwardly railing at himself for bringing Abernathy along, Finn nodded and pushed Yost toward Zach. "Call for assistance. We have to go."

Zach nodded. "Backup is on the way. Oh, and here's Reed Branson. We've got it from here—just go."

Once again Finn lifted his K-9 partner into his arms, tears stinging his vision. If anything happened to his K-9 partner, he'd never forgive himself.

SEVENTEEN

The blood coating Abernathy's rear flank was horrifying. Eva held the chocolate Lab puppy against her chest while placing her other hand over Abernathy's wound in a lame attempt to stop the bleeding. As they left the alley, Eva glanced around, then released Abernathy long enough to flag a passing squad car. The patrol car slowed to a stop. She rushed forward and bent down to look at the pair of officers inside. "K-9 officer injured," she managed between hacking coughs. "We need a ride to the vet."

"Sure. Get in." The passenger-side officer gestured with his hand.

Eva didn't hesitate to open the door for Finn. Still cradling Abernathy to his chest, he awkwardly slid inside. She closed the door behind him, then went around to get in on the other side. She was relieved that Cocoa was content to sit in her lap.

The officer driving the squad was on the radio,

informing the dispatcher about the need to drive an injured K-9 for care. Afterward, the cop caught her gaze in the rearview mirror. "Where's the vet?"

Eva glanced helplessly at Finn. He lifted his tortured gaze to hers.

"There's an emergency veterinary clinic in Jackson Heights near our K-9 headquarters." Finn's voice was low and husky with emotion.

"Got it." The officer behind the wheel hit the lights and gunned the engine. "What happened?"

Finn didn't answer, his attention laser focused on Abernathy. She could hear him murmuring words of encouragement to his partner. Eva rested her hand on Abernathy's silky fur, hoping and praying he'd be okay, then caught the driver's gaze in the mirror again.

"He was grazed by a bullet, then kicked by a suspect on his wounded flank." She coughed again, wondering if she would sound like a heavy smoker for the rest of her life after being trapped in the fire.

"Man, that's terrible," the officer commiserated. "Hope the jerk rots in prison for a long time. I'll do my best to get you to Jackson Heights soon as possible."

Finn buried his face against his partner's coat, and she knew he was beating himself up over Abernathy's aggravated injury. But the showdown at the training center was her fault more so than Finn's.

Abernathy had been put in harm's way because she'd allowed her boss to dupe her, taking her from safety at gunpoint. Why hadn't she understood that Wade Yost was part of the drug-dealing operation from the very beginning? Looking back, Wade's involvement made sense. Obviously, he was the one who'd exposed Malina to a life of crime. Lured her with easy money and likely convinced her to try their so-called merchandise. Maybe the painkillers she'd taken after her surgery had set her up for switching to cocaine. Eva had heard that it was all too easy to become addicted, that one hit was all it took.

Sadly, she could envision exactly how it must have happened. After things fell apart, Yost had fired her sister. Maybe that was when she'd stolen their package.

If only Malina had come to her for help. Or to Pete. The sister she knew would never have put her son's safety at risk.

Yet that was exactly what Malina had done.

No one spoke for several long minutes. The only noise inside the vehicle was static-filled voices coming through the radio. Eva realized that she could ask the vet to check Cocoa for signs of injury, too. The poor puppy didn't look injured from being stuck with the stinky guy for the past four going on five days, but she wouldn't rest until she knew there were no internal injuries or issues with smoke inhalation, as well.

"Do you have an address for the vet?" the driver asked, breaking the silence. "We're approaching Jackson Heights now."

Finn lifted his head and provided directions to the emergency veterinary clinic a few blocks down from the K-9 headquarters.

When they pulled up in front of the emergency veterinary clinic, Eva had to wait for the officer to let them out of the back seat. She and Finn, along with their respective dogs, went inside.

Finn hit the emergency buzzer with his elbow. "Injured K-9 officer! I need help!"

A veterinary assistant instantly came out through the door separating the front waiting room from the back clinical area. "What's the problem?"

"Abernathy was nicked by a bullet, then brutally kicked."

The tech's eyes widened. "I'll get the vet right away."

Twenty seconds later, a slender woman with curly red hair wearing a long white lab coat emerged through the doorway. "I'm Dr. Yncz Dubois." Her French accent was charming, but Eva could tell Finn didn't notice. "Bring your K-9 officer this way."

Eva wanted to speak up about Cocoa but held

back, understanding that Abernathy's wound was more serious.

She settled down to wait, lightly stroking Cocoa's fur while fighting the urge to cough. Her elbow and hip were bruised from hitting the floor on Finn's command. She'd sacrificed her body to make sure Cocoa was safe. She murmured a prayer of thanks that God had watched over them.

The veterinary tech came out a few minutes later. "My name is Anna Lee. Does your puppy also need to be seen?"

While it wasn't exactly an emergency, she was here and liked Dr. Dubois. "Yes. This puppy was taken from the guide dog training center four—well, now five—days ago and I'm concerned they mistreated him during that time. He was also stuck in a fire with me and could have smoke inhalation." She coughed, then continued, "I'd appreciate it if Dr. Dubois would check him out for me when she's finished with Abernathy."

"Of course." Anna crouched beside Eva's chair and held out her hand for Cocoa to sniff. "You're a good boy, aren't you, Cocoa?" She crooned. "And such a lovely name."

"He's learning to be a guide dog," Eva said as Anna gently took Cocoa from her arms. "He led me out of a burning house. I didn't see any burns on his coat, but if you could ask Dr. Dubois to check out his lungs, I'd appreciate it."

"I will. Although your lungs don't sound great, either." Anna stood, looking down at her.

"I know." She managed to smile while holding off yet another cough. "Thank you."

Anna disappeared through the doorway, and moments later Finn returned to the waiting room. His face was grim and gaunt, the wound on his temple caked with blood. Her heart ached for him.

"Abernathy is going to be fine," she assured him.

He nodded and dropped into the chair beside her. Leaning forward, he propped his elbows on his knees and cradled his head in his hands.

"Finn, don't." She stroked a hand down his back. "It's not your fault. It's mine. I never suspected Wade Yost of being involved. When he stuck that gun in my side and ordered me to leave... I didn't know what else to do."

Finn lifted his head. He shifted in his seat and put his arm around her shoulders, drawing her close. "I'm sorry you had to go through that. I should have figured out the truth sooner. I had no idea Grant Ulrich owned the guide dog training center. And Abernathy's injury isn't our fault— it sits with Ulrich and Greer."

She rested her head on his shoulder, reveling in his comforting scent. Now that the danger was over and the bad guys had been captured, she knew that her time with Finn had come to an end. It was heartbreaking, even though she understood it was for the best.

"Officer Gallagher?"

Finn straightened quickly when Dr. Dubois called his name. "Yes?"

"I need to do a minor surgical procedure on Abernathy. He's bleeding internally, and I need to find the source and cauterize it."

"Surgery?" She felt Finn's muscles tense with anxiety.

Dr. Dubois smiled gently. "It won't take long. Abernathy is in perfect shape. I don't expect to encounter any problems or complications."

"Do it." Finn's voice was low and raspy. "Take care of my partner."

"I will. And when I'm finished with Abernathy I'll check out the chocolate Lab."

"Thank you." Eva wasn't sure the vet heard as she disappeared behind the closed door.

"Surgery," Finn whispered.

"It's okay. As Dr. Dubois said, Abernathy is strong and healthy. He's going to do fine."

Finn surprised her by turning and leaning on her for support. He wrapped his arms around her and buried his face in her hair. "If he doesn't make it…" He couldn't finish.

She clutched him close, in awe that the big strong Finn Gallagher was seeking support from her. "He will. We'll pray for God to watch over him."

"**Dear Lord, please keep Abernathy safe in**

Your care." Finn's anguished whisper resonated deep within.

"And Cocoa, too. Amen," she added, then ruined the moment by coughing. Finn didn't seem to mind. He only clutched her closer.

They stayed like that for a long time, finding comfort and support in each other's arms.

"Officer Gallagher?"

At the sound of his name, Finn forced himself to let go of Eva long enough to turn toward the vet. "Is he okay?"

The pretty redhead smiled and nodded. "He tolerated the procedure very well. He'll need to stay here overnight, but barring any complications, he'll be discharged into your care tomorrow morning."

A wave of relief washed over him. "Good. Thank you."

"You're welcome." Dr. Dubois glanced at Eva. "I've examined Cocoa, too, and have some lab tests pending. He looks a little malnourished and dehydrated, but I don't see anything more serious. His lungs sound okay, too. I've given him a fluid bolus—you'll see the bulge in the back of his neck—and have given him some moist dog food. He only ate a small amount, so over the next few days I want you to feed him three times a day. I need a little more time for the tests to come back, then he'll be ready for discharge, too."

Malnourished and dehydrated. The words made anger burn in his gut all over again. First Abernathy, now Cocoa. The little pup had proved his worth helping to get Eva out of the burning house. Greer and Ulrich didn't value human or animal life, and frankly, he couldn't wait to testify against those jerks at trial.

"I don't have any wet dog food at home. You'll have to tell me what kind to get."

It was on the tip of his tongue to point out she didn't have a home, but there was time to worry about where she'd spend the night later.

"Not a problem." Dr. Dubois waved a hand. "I'll send you home with samples. Once those are gone, you can switch back to dry food. I'm sure he'll get his appetite back in no time."

Eva nodded but didn't say anything more. Her coughing seemed to be getting better, but he still wanted her to get medical care.

"I'll get you to the hospital soon," he promised.

"No need. My cough isn't as bad as it was."

Stubborn woman. When the vet left them alone, Finn drew Eva into his arms. She hugged him, resting her cheek on his chest.

She felt perfect in his arms, and in that moment he knew he didn't want to lose her. Ironic how he hadn't thought twice about moving on from one no-strings-attached relationship to the next without realizing what he truly wanted. What he needed.

The thought of losing Eva made his heart squeeze tightly in his chest, making it impossible to breathe. Lifting her chin with his finger, he lowered his mouth to hers, kissing her with all the love he felt inside.

Their kiss lingered for long, breathless moments until she broke away from him. She placed her hand on his chest, gasping for breath in a way that made her cough again. "We shouldn't do this," she managed.

"Because of your cough? I know, I'll take you to the hospital soon."

"Not because of that." She rolled her eyes.

"Then why not?" Finn didn't understand. "The danger is over, Eva. We have everyone in custody. Thanks to you, we've busted up the drug ring once and for all."

"I'm glad about that. Truly." The way she avoided his gaze bothered him. "But we can't be together, Finn. As you said, the danger is over. It's time for you to move on." She lifted her face to his. "Isn't that what you do? Isn't that what has made the Gallagher charm so famous among the other K-9 cops?"

"Not this time." He looked deep into her beautiful blue eyes, trying to think of a way to convince her. "I don't want to move on, Eva. I want you. To be with you. Because I love you. When I realized you were still inside the fire… I nearly lost my mind."

Her smile was sad and she shook her head. "You might think you love me, Finn, but that feeling will fade over time along with my eyesight. You have your whole life ahead of you. You'll find someone else to love. Someone that won't be legally blind in the next few years."

"You're wrong about me, Eva." He couldn't help being upset by her attitude.

"I already had one boyfriend who dropped me because of my diagnosis. I'd rather not go through that again." When he opened his mouth to argue, she lifted a hand to stop him. "Besides, I'm not wrong about your track record with women."

That stopped him because it was true. "Yeah, okay. Until I met you, I wasn't interested in commitment. Cops aren't good husbands or fathers. My mom—" He grimaced, then forced himself to tell her the truth. "Let's just say she couldn't stand being married to a cop. She and my dad fought all the time, until one day she up and left. I was eight years old." The memory of that day had faded over time, but the sense of loss had never left him. "I didn't see her again until I was an adult. No Christmas presents, no birthday cards. Nothing."

Eva gasped and clutched his arms. "Finn. That's horrible!"

He shrugged. "It wasn't easy. But me and my dad became really close. He was a good man and a great cop. I was proud to follow in his footsteps."

"Your mom… Do you think something happened to her?" Eva asked. "I can't believe she'd just disappear from your life like that."

"Not knowing bothered me, so I looked for her. Found her about ten years ago in New Jersey. She's remarried and has two kids. Her husband left the house wearing a business suit, so I figure he's a lawyer or an accountant. Something safe. The complete opposite of a cop."

"Her loss. I think you're amazing, Finn." Eva tightened her grip on his arms, then released him. "Your dedication to protecting the people of New York, to upholding the law, is honorable. Don't let anyone ever tell you otherwise. You're a good cop and a good man just like your dad. Your mother was wrong to leave like she did." She tilted her head to the side. "What did she say when she saw you?"

"She didn't." It was his turn to avoid her gaze. "I didn't bother talking to her. She made her choice. I watched her interact with her new family for a while, then turned and walked away."

"Oh, Finn." Eva sighed. "You deserve so much better."

That made him smile. "You're right about that, Eva." He drew her close again. "I deserve you."

Her internal struggle played across her features. Ironically, it gave him hope knowing that she was protesting more because of her impending blindness than a lack of returning his feelings.

Although he desperately wanted to hear her say the words, he silently vowed to be patient.

"I don't know what to do with you," she finally said.

"You could try giving me a chance. To prove I'm better than your loser boyfriend." Now he understood why she didn't trust any man could love her, knowing of her progressive vision loss. But he did. "I love you, Eva Kendall. And I'm happy to spend the rest of my life showing you just how much."

"I love you, too, Finn." Her confession made his heart soar and he swept her up against him, sealing their fate with another kiss.

"Um, excuse me?" The sound of Dr. Dubois's voice broke them apart. "I have Cocoa ready for you to take home."

"Thank you." Eva crossed the room to gather the puppy close. Cocoa licked her face, then greeted Finn exuberantly. The fluids and food had done wonders for the pup.

"Could I see Abernathy before I leave?" Finn asked.

"Of course. But understand he's still a bit sedated."

Finn followed the vet into the back, where he could see Abernathy lying in a crate. There was a small line of stitches along his flank from the procedure. When Abernathy caught his scent, the dog lifted his head but didn't have the energy to hold it there. His tail thumped twice, then went still.

"It's okay, boy." Finn stroked Abernathy's coat. "You're going to be fine. I'll come in the morning to bust you out of here, okay?"

Abernathy's tail thumped again. Finn felt the sting of tears in his eyes and blinked them away. He bent down to press a kiss on top of Abernathy's head, then left, knowing Abernathy was in good hands.

In the waiting room, he took Eva's hand before turning to face the vet. "What time can I pick him up tomorrow?"

"Anytime. We're open all night, remember?" Dr. Dubois smiled.

"Right. Then I'll be here at eight." *Maybe earlier*, he added silently. He escorted Eva and Cocoa outside, then stopped, realizing he didn't have his SUV.

As if on cue, his phone buzzed. Zach Jameson. "How's Abernathy?"

"Healing from surgery. Where are you?"

"At headquarters with Reed Branson. I told Noah about what happened with your partner. He'll be glad to hear Abernathy will be okay. But we have Greer and Ulrich here. I figured you'd want to be here while we question these guys."

He did indeed, and he glanced at Eva. She looked exhausted. "Pick me up at the vet. We'll drop Eva and Cocoa off at my place, then we'll head back to interrogate these guys."

"Be there in five."

"Your place?" Eva pinned him with a narrow glare. "Isn't that a bit presumptuous?"

"I have to work for several hours yet, so I won't be there. Or there's a hotel not far that I could take you to." He hesitated, then added, "Unless you want to go back to Pete's house?"

"No, it's too late. I wouldn't want to risk waking Mikey." She sighed. "I guess that leaves me no alternative other than to take you up on that hotel. Just make sure it's a dog-friendly one as I'm bringing Cocoa."

"I will." He was relieved she'd be close by. Now he just needed to find a way to convince her that a quick engagement and even quicker wedding was the way to go.

But first, he needed to finish the case.

For Abernathy's sake and his own.

EIGHTEEN

Eva awoke the next morning with a sore throat, but the incessant coughing seemed to have disappeared. The room wasn't at all familiar, and then she realized that she was in a hotel near Finn's home.

Cocoa was curled up beside her on the bed. The poor puppy had been so afraid to be separated from her, she'd given in and allowed the puppy to sleep with her.

Cocoa sensed her movements and jumped up excitedly. Eva took the animal outside, then cleaned up after him. Although it was early, she found herself wondering what time Finn might show up.

She hadn't expected to fall asleep after everything that had transpired. But somehow the memory of Finn's kiss and his declaration of love had brought a sense of comfort. Knowing the bad guys had been arrested had helped provide another layer of security.

God had certainly watched over them last night.

Two minutes after she returned to her room, there was a knock at her door. When she opened it, Finn stood there, looking amazingly handsome.

"Hey!" He bent to give her a quick kiss, then flashed a distracted smile. "Ready to go? I'm making breakfast at my place before we pick up Abernathy."

"Um, sure. I guess." She glanced around the hotel room, found her purse, then saw the cans of wet dog food. She hadn't had a can opener with her so she decided to take it along to Finn's. Last, she picked up Cocoa. "Okay, we're ready."

"Great." Finn ushered her outside and drove them the short distance to his place. When they entered the kitchen, which was surprisingly spotlessly clean, he began pulling out pots and pans.

"Do you need anything? I'm not completely helpless in the kitchen."

"Never said you were," Finn responded. "Have a seat—this won't take long. As soon as we're finished, I'd like to get over to the vet."

She understood his need to see Abernathy. "Okay. What happened last night? Anything you can tell me that won't jeopardize your case?"

He quirked an eyebrow. "How many cops have you dated?"

"Huh?" Had she missed something? "None. Why?"

"It's amazing that you seem to understand what

a cop's life entails, that we can't always talk about our cases. I noticed from the moment we first met how you seemed to think like a cop."

She hesitated, then confessed, "I had an uncle who was a cop. My mom's brother. Uncle Jerry. He was my favorite uncle and my mother used to tease me about how much I loved hearing his stories, even the ones I'd listened to over and over. He passed away two years ago, and I still miss him."

"I knew you had to have had some exposure to police," he joked. "Where are your parents?"

"They moved to Arizona. I usually see them a few times a year."

"Hopefully in the winter, right?"

"Right." Her smile faded. "At first I thought of becoming a cop, then decided I was more interested in healing people, so I studied nursing. When Malina was diagnosed with retinitis pigmentosa, the same way our mother had been, I instinctively knew I would have it, too. So I dropped out of nursing school and began training guide dogs. I was diagnosed four months ago."

Finn's expression turned serious. "Eva, I know how difficult it must be for you, but please know that I love you no matter what diagnosis you have. Either one of us could come down with some sort of illness. Cancer, diabetes, heart disease. You name it, it's out there."

She knew he was right, but still believed he

was glossing over the reality of her future. "Yes, but being blind is a big deal. It will make having a family impossible."

"Impossible? Not hardly." Finn came over to sit beside her. He took her hands in his. "Challenging? Maybe. But not impossible. The Eva Kendall I know won't let anything stand in the way of what she wants."

That made her chuckle even though she knew he was still taking it all too lightly. "Right now she wants breakfast, so hurry it up, will you? I need to feed Cocoa."

Finn stole another quick kiss and then returned to his frying pan. She opened the can of food the vet had provided and spooned it into a bowl for Cocoa. Reassured by the way the chocolate Lab ate with enthusiasm, she knew the puppy would be fine.

When Finn had their eggs and toast ready, he set the platter on the table, then reached for her hand. "Dear Lord, we thank You for this food we are about to eat. We also thank You for keeping us safe in Your care and healing our wounds. We ask that You continue to guide us on Your chosen path as we get married, have children and live happily ever after. Amen."

"Amen," she answered automatically, then jerked her head up to look at him. "Wait, what? Are you crazy?"

"Crazy in love," he assured her. "And if you're

not ready to accept my proposal yet, that's fine. I'll ask every day until you say yes."

"Every day?" She laughed, which then turned into a coughing fit. "Did you get any sleep last night? I think your brain cells have gone on the fritz."

"Four hours, and my brain cells are firing just fine." He squeezed her hand gently, then let go so they could eat. As if he hadn't just proposed, he went on. "After we pick up Abernathy, I'd like to drop by Pete's house to let him know he and Mikey are safe. Oh, and there's an award ceremony next week that I hope you'll attend with me. The brass is giving Abernathy a medal of honor for being wounded in the line of duty."

"So soon?"

"I guess. I thought they'd wait until the K-9 graduation ceremony, but that won't be for six months." He shrugged. "Guess they didn't want to wait that long."

"Okay." Her head was spinning with all the plans Finn was making. Had she imagined his proposal? During a prayer, no less? Goofy man.

They finished their breakfast in under twenty minutes. Finn filled two cups of coffee in to-go mugs and led the way outside to his K-9 SUV. She kept Cocoa with her as she slid in beside Finn.

The trip to the vet didn't take long. When they walked in, she thought for sure she could hear **Abernathy** barking.

"Calm down," the assistant said, bringing Abernathy out from the back. The poor yellow Lab was wearing the cone of shame and obviously didn't like it. "Here you go."

"Thanks." Finn took Abernathy's leash and dropped to one knee, giving the animal a good rub. "Sorry about the cone, but hopefully those sutures will heal up fast. We'll get rid of that thing as soon as possible, okay?"

Abernathy stared up at him with mournful brown eyes, as if to ask, *Why not now?*

"You're a brave boy." Eva scratched him behind the ears. "I bet Mikey will be happy to see you. And Cocoa, too."

"Next stop, Pete's," Finn agreed.

Eva couldn't deny feeling a bit apprehensive about seeing her brother-in-law again. So much had happened in the short time since she'd left him and Mikey. Logically she knew that Pete didn't hold a grudge against her for Mikey being in danger; at the same time, she knew their relationship might be strained for a while.

Still, she adored Mikey and knew Pete would need help, more so now that Malina was gone.

She prayed that Pete would find solace in God.

Finn parked in Pete's driveway, then went around to the back to let Abernathy out. The K-9 still looked unhappy about the cone, but he didn't try to get it off. Eva carried Cocoa. As they approached the front door, she heard voices from the backyard.

"Pete? Mikey?" she called as she leaned over to the fence. There was a door with a latch on it leading to the backyard. "It's Eva and Finn. We have Abernathy and Cocoa."

"Cocoa?" Mikey's excited voice made her grin. "I wanna see Cocoa!"

"Come on in," Pete called.

Eva lifted the latch and opened the gate. They went into the small backyard to find Pete and Mikey sitting near the turtle-shaped sandbox.

"Cocoa!" Mikey was excited to see the puppy. "You found him!"

"Sure did." She met Pete's gaze and gave a brief nod. "Cocoa is safe now. And so are we."

"We locked all the bad guys in jail," Finn added.

"What happened to Abernathy?" Pete's gaze was troubled.

"Grazed, and then kicked, but he'll be okay." She was glad Finn didn't go into details with Mr. Big Ears listening. "I wanted to let you know personally that you're safe."

"The package?" Pete asked.

Eva glanced at Finn, who shrugged. "We may never know what happened to it. But the guys in jail know that we don't have it, so I don't think there's a reason to worry. The rest of the operation is going down as we speak."

Pete's brow furrowed, but he didn't say anything.

Cocoa jumped into the sandbox with Mikey, making the little boy giggle. "I love Cocoa," he announced.

The puppy began digging in the corner of the sandbox farthest from the house. Curious, Eva went over to see what Cocoa had found. When she saw a hint of plastic, she knew.

The package.

"Finn! Come quick!"

Finn was beside her in an instant. "What in the world?" He knelt down, easing Cocoa aside to finish uncovering the package.

"Is that—" She didn't finish.

"Cocaine," Finn said grimly. He looked at her, then shifted his gaze to Pete. "It was here all along."

Eva let out a low groan. "I never thought to look out here."

"Me, either." Finn hefted the package in his hand. "Looks and weighs about as much as a ten-pound bag of sugar. This is worth a lot of money to those guys."

"Fifty grand," she whispered. "That's what Greer claimed."

"Not worth dying over," Pete said, a faint note of bitterness lacing his tone.

"No, it's not," Finn agreed. "I'm sorry."

Pete blew out a heavy breath. "Not your fault. Just…do me a favor and get it out of here, okay?

I can't stand knowing that Malina died because of those drugs."

"Sure." Finn carried the newfound evidence to his SUV, leaving Pete and Eva and Mikey alone in the backyard.

"I'm sorry, too, Pete," she said, breaking the silence. "I hope you'll let me know when you need me to watch Mikey."

He hesitated, shrugged, then nodded. "I appreciate that, Eva. I've been sitting here, berating myself for going to that stupid conference in Atlanta. I hate to admit it, but at the time, I was anxious to get away from it all. But the thought of losing Mikey scared me to death. I need to spend more time with him, and even more so, we need grief counseling. We have to learn how to cope with losing Malina. I've been granted an official leave of absence for two weeks and can use my vacation time to extend it if needed. I'll let you know when I return to work."

"I'm so glad to hear that, Pete. You and Mikey are going to be fine." She bent over and gave Mikey a hug and a kiss. "See you later, alligator," she teased.

"After a while, crocodile!" Mikey shouted back.

Eva carried Cocoa through the gate to where Finn and Abernathy waited near the SUV. She heard him on the phone, no doubt calling in about the drugs. When he saw her, he finished his call and slid the phone in his pocket.

"Everything okay?"

"It will be," she said with confidence. "Pete's strong enough to get through this. He's a good father and will do what's best for Mikey."

"I need to drop this evidence at headquarters. Do you want me to drop you off at the hotel or my place for a bit?"

"Um." His place? Was he serious? First an off-the-cuff proposal and now this?

She was tempted to pinch herself to make sure she wasn't dreaming. The future Finn offered was one she couldn't have.

Or bear to lose.

Finn hid a smile at Eva's poorly masked confusion. He hadn't been joking when he'd asked her to marry him, and he silently promised to prove it by taking her ring shopping as soon as he wrapped this up.

Eva had requested to go to the hotel, but he wasn't thrilled with that idea. Even though she was safe, he didn't like having her out of his sight.

At headquarters, Finn quickly flagged down Zach Jameson. "We found it."

"What?" Zach's puzzled gaze cleared instantly. "The package? Are you kidding? Where?"

"Buried in Mikey's sandbox."

Zach let out a disgusted snort. "I should have had Eddie sniffing around back there. It makes sense now that you think about it. Of course she didn't keep it inside the house. Buried in the sand-box was a perfect hiding place."

"I know. Have they given us anything else?"

Zach nodded. "Names of other players. This is it, Finn. We broke the biggest drug ring in New York City."

"I'm glad."

"I heard Abernathy is getting a medal of honor next week." Zach patted Abernathy's head. "You're going to take the cone off for pictures, right?"

"Right," Finn agreed. "I'll check in with you later, okay?"

"Sure thing."

Finn was making his way through the maze of cubicles when one of his fellow cops, Gavin Sutherland, snagged his arm.

"Finn. Have a minute?"

"Sure. What's up?"

Gavin's expression was grim. "Remember the building that came down due to a boiler explosion a few months ago?"

"Yeah, what about it?"

"I think it's connected to my newest case. The newspaper reported the source of the explosion was the boiler, but I've recently learned the source was really a bomb. The place was blown up on purpose."

Finn's eyes widened. "That's not good."

"No, it isn't." Gavin glanced down at his K-9

partner. "Tommy is the best bomb-sniffing dog on the force, so we're being pulled in to help. I may need backup."

Tommy was a springer spaniel who specialized in finding bombs.

"Let me know and we'll be there to help. You and Tommy need to be careful, Gavin."

"We will."

Finn left headquarters, returning to find Eva and Cocoa waiting outside headquarters in the shade. She was stunningly beautiful, but that wasn't why he loved her.

He loved her spirit, her determination, her independence, her wit, her spunk. He loved everything about her. "Hey, sorry about that. It took longer than I thought."

"Not a problem. Listen, let's just sit at Griffin's for a while. I don't want to be stuck in my hotel room longer than I need to be."

"Okay, I'm up for that," Finn agreed. He gazed into her blue eyes for a long moment, then said, "Eva, I love you so much. I promise to be a good husband and a good father to our children. Will you please marry me?"

She stared at him. "You said you'd propose once a day, not once every couple of hours," she accused.

"I lied." He swept her close and kissed her, longer this time, trying to prove how much he cared. "I'm sorry, but I can't seem to help myself.

You better get used to it. These proposals keep popping up before I can stop them. I'll ask until I wear you down."

She laughed and shook her head. "You already have, Finn. Yes."

His eyebrows levered up, hope shining in his eyes. "Yes—what?"

"Yes, I love you. Yes, I'll marry you. Yes, I'll have a family with you."

"She said yes!" Finn scooped her up against him, with Cocoa sandwiched between them, and spun her in a circle. "Thank you for making me the happiest man in the world!"

She didn't answer, but that might have been because he was kissing her again.

Finn had her right where he wanted her. And now that he had her in his arms, he knew he'd never let her go.

* * * * *

If you enjoyed Blind Trust, *look for
Gavin and Brianne's story,* Deep Undercover,
*coming up next and the rest of the
True Blue K-9 Unit series from
Love Inspired Suspense.*

True Blue K-9 Unit:
These police officers fight for justice with the help of their brave canine partners.

Dear Reader,

I was blessed and honored to be given the opportunity to participate in this True Blue K-9 Unit continuity. It's been amazing working with this fantastic group of talented authors.

I've visited New York City many times and had fun researching the Queens area, but please know that any errors are strictly my own.

I hope you enjoyed Finn and Eva's story. And if you're wondering about Pete and Mikey, don't worry, you'll meet them again later this year in my *True Blue K-9 Unit Christmas* novella!

As always, I love hearing from my readers. Please drop me a note through my website at www.laurascottbooks.com, or message me through my Facebook page at Laura Scott Author. I'm also on Twitter @laurascottbooks.

Yours in faith,
Laura Scott

Get 4 FREE REWARDS!

We'll send you 2 FREE Books plus 2 FREE Mystery Gifts.

Love Inspired® books feature contemporary inspirational romances with Christian characters facing the challenges of life and love.

FREE Value Over **$20**

YES! Please send me 2 FREE Love Inspired® Romance novels and my 2 FREE mystery gifts (gifts are worth about $10 retail). After receiving them, if I don't wish to receive any more books, I can return the shipping statement marked "cancel." If I don't cancel, I will receive 6 brand-new novels every month and be billed just $5.24 for the regular-print edition or $5.74 each for the larger-print edition in the U.S., or $5.74 each for the regular-print edition or $6.24 each for the larger-print edition in Canada. That's a savings of at least 13% off the cover price. It's quite a bargain! Shipping and handling is just 50¢ per book in the U.S. and 75¢ per book in Canada.* I understand that accepting the 2 free books and gifts places me under no obligation to buy anything. I can always return a shipment and cancel at any time. The free books and gifts are mine to keep no matter what I decide.

Choose one: ☐ **Love Inspired® Romance Regular-Print**
(105/305 IDN GMY4)

☐ **Love Inspired® Romance Larger-Print**
(122/322 IDN GMY4)

Name (please print)

Address   Apt. #

City   State/Province   Zip/Postal Code

Mail to the Reader Service:
IN U.S.A.: P.O. Box 1341, Buffalo, NY 14240-8531
IN CANADA: P.O. Box 603, Fort Erie, Ontario L2A 5X3

Want to try 2 free books from another series! Call 1-800-873-8635 or visit www.ReaderService.com.

---

*Terms and prices subject to change without notice. Prices do not include sales taxes, which will be charged (if applicable) based on your state or country of residence. Canadian residents will be charged applicable taxes. Offer not valid in Quebec. This offer is limited to one order per household. Books received may not be as shown. Not valid for current subscribers to Love Inspired Romance books. All orders subject to approval. Credit or debit balances in a customer's account(s) may be offset by any other outstanding balance owed by or to the customer. Please allow 4 to 6 weeks for delivery. Offer available while quantities last.

Your Privacy—The Reader Service is committed to protecting your privacy. Our Privacy Policy is available online at www.ReaderService.com or upon request from the Reader Service. We make a portion of our mailing list available to reputable third parties that offer products we believe may interest you. If you prefer that we not exchange your name with third parties, or if you wish to clarify or modify your communication preferences, please visit us at www.ReaderService.com/consumerschoice or write to us at Reader Service Preference Service, P.O. Box 9062, Buffalo, NY 14240-9062. Include your complete name and address.

LI19R2

READERSERVICE.COM

Manage your account online!

- Review your order history
- Manage your payments
- Update your address

We've designed the Reader Service website just for you.

Enjoy all the features!

- Discover new series available to you, and read excerpts from any series.
- Respond to mailings and special monthly offers.
- Browse the Bonus Bucks catalog and online-only exculsives.
- Share your feedback.

Visit us at:

ReaderService.com

RS16R